"I am in love," said Lord Farr, "with the beautiful, incomparable Miss Stansfield, who is currently deciding whether she will marry me or my cousin Rex, the eleventh Duke of Broxbridge. He has now taken an unfair advantage of me by inviting her and her mother to his estate in the hope that her grasping parent will influence Miss Stansfield to favor his suit when she sees his ancient castle and vast acreage."

"I cannot think that Miss Stansfield will be moved to agree with her mother," Meriel protested.

"I intend to see that she does not," Lord Farr replied, a twinkle flickering briefly in his eyes. "Miss Stansfield, you see, is very sensitive, has a lively imagination and, once frightened, might regard the castle with dread and horror. Fortunately for me, the castle has a legend. It is said that the ghost of a girl wronged by one of Rex's ancestors walks its halls. The Lady Blue, she is called, for she is dressed in blue, has blue skin, eyes—and blue hair . . .

# Lady Blue

## Zabrina Faire

WARNER BOOKS

A Warner Communications Company

WARNER BOOKS EDITION

ISBN 0-446-94056-6

Cover art by Walter Popp

Warner Books, Inc., 75 Rockefeller Plaza,
New York, N.Y. 10019

 A Warner Communications Company

Printed in the United States of America

Not associated with Warner Press, Inc., of Anderson, Indiana

First Printing: April, 1979

10 9 8 7 6 5 4 3 2 1

# (1)

Sunrise, turning the London sky a golden orange, was reflected in the little pools of rain water lying at intervals along South Street. Miss Meriel Hathaway, slipping between the Ionic columns that fronted the doorway of Lord Lithwaite's mansion, raised her face to the fresh breeze gratefully. Its coolness was restoring after the heat of her small, airless chamber. She hurried along the flagged walk to the gates, unlatched them, then let herself out. Standing with her back against the carefully closed cool iron gates, she looked about her with delight. The dawn gave promise of becoming a lovely day, and since neither her pupil nor his parent would be astir, she had a full three hours in which to enjoy it!

Her only problem was destination. Should

she walk up South Street or venture into the tantalizing mass of greenery that was Hyde Park? From where she stood, Meriel could see the trees garbed in new spring coats of pale leaves and ravishing pink blossoms. The Park was not unfamiliar to her. She had walked in it with Lord Algernon—or rather, ran—following his zigzag progress as carefully as she could. Endeavoring not to lose sight of him, nervously praying that he would not hide from her, as he had done on more than one occasion, leaving her to dash back to the house in fear and trembling only to find him grinning wickedly at her when she ventured inside. She detached her gaze from the park, wishing she could as easily detach her mind from Lord Algernon.

"I have three hours." She reminded herself resolutely. "Three hours in which to be me—Meriel Hathaway, young lady of . . ." She smiled derisively. Not even in her imagination could she add the word "fashion." She was not a young lady of fashion. She was a governess; had been one for four and a half months and, as far as she knew, might be one for the rest of her life. At that thought, she drooped and instinctively moved away from the gates of Lithwaite Mansion, turning up the street, oblivious of her direction. Her pleasure in the beauty of the sky had vanished; instead, eyes sadly turned to the ground, she was thinking of the past and of the promises that had remained unfulfilled.

"If I had known . . . would I have . . . ?" She whispered to herself and conjured up a vision of Lord Lithwaite, at the moment he had arrived at the small cottage she and her father, Sir Sylvian Hathaway, occupied in the town of Chalfont St. Giles. She had been sitting by her father's bedside trying to coax him to sip a little of the gruel she had prepared, when Sally, their maid-of-all-work, had come up to tell her that there was ever-so-elegant a gentleman waiting in their front parlor.

He had certainly been elegant and handsome, in well-fitting clothes, a wonderfully intricate snowy cravat, tight dark trousers and brightly polished Hessian boots. The multitiered cape that proclaimed him a Corinthian lay carelessly draped over a chair. Meriel had never seen a member of the *beau monde* up close. Although her father, a baronet, could have had entrée to those circles, his estate had been gambled away by a guardian uncle before he had reached his majority. Consequently his income was tiny. Furthermore, being a man of a reclusive nature, he was quite content to remain in his library. There, he labored over his book, *Milton's Paradise*, which was a carefully annotated description of the town in which they lived, as it had been when the famous poet Milton fled from plague-stricken London to live there and finish *Paradise Lost* and write *Paradise Regained*.

It had been Meriel who had done much looking into archives and old records and interviewing descendants of those who had resided at Chalfont St. Giles during the seventeenth century. This research had been extremely time-consuming, more so in the final two years of Sir Sylvian's life, when he had worked feverishly to finish the work before he died. He had not been successful. She sighed. It was a pity he had not expended his energy on his own poems. As a youth, he had penned charming and elegant poetry, but had not written a line of verse for many years.

Meriel blamed that on the tragic, early death of her mother. Up until her sixth birthday, her father had been a much different man: gay, smiling, always whistling. The gaiety, the smiles, and the whistling had all ceased on the morning that Lady Milicent Hathaway, hurrying across High Street with the doll she had purchased for her little daughter, had waved gaily at Sir Sylvian, who was standing on the other side. As she started recklessly across the road, a curricle had suddenly appeared from nowhere and run her down. Trampled and broken, the lovely lady had survived only a few moments, just long enough to smile briefly at her agonized young husband and murmur a regretful farewell.

Sir Sylvian had been unable to keep from reproaching his daughter for her mother's death. Many a sentence during Meriel's years of growing up had begun "If she'd not gone to purchase that doll . . ." Yet, at the same time, Sir Sylvian had given her a good education at home in subjects few women of her day understood. For, if he had not loved her, he had respected an inquiring mind that was much like his own.

Meriel was proficient in Greek, Latin, French, and Italian. Under her father's tutelage, she had delved into history, geography, science, politics, and, of course, Milton. She could ride and swim, because, until his illness, those had been the two pursuits her father enjoyed.

However, as she discovered when she came to the Lithwaite house, her education had been, in some respects, sadly neglected. Aside from the household chores their straitened circumstances had required she do, Meriel knew little of such womanly pursuits as china-painting, sketching, needlepoint, or embroidery. She could not play the pianoforte or the harp, and, unlike other girls of eighteen, she had never been to an assembly or a ball; but that was just as well, for she could not dance.

If her background was odd for a genteel young woman, it had pleased Lord Lithwaite, whose brief meeting with his friend had convinced him that his life hung on the merest thread. He had discussed his daughter's future with Sir Sylvian, and learned that Hathaway's small income would cease with his death; leaving Meriel destitute. The sick man, brought to a tardy realization of her plight, had been much concerned. Lord Lithwaite had soothed his friend's last hours by promising to see the girl well established in his own household as governess to his son. "However," he had assured Sir Sylvian, "she will be treated as one of the family." It was a promise that he had repeated to Meriel.

Not for the first time, his words echoed through her mind: "You will want for nothing, dear child, and the teaching of my son Algernon will not be arduous. He is a bright child and though he is a bit high-spirited, I am sure you will be able to cope with that. You seem an eminently sensible young woman."

She had thanked him shyly for his praise and, as the days progressed, had other reasons to be grateful to him. For, in addition to settling her future for her, Lord Lithwaite had remained in town to comfort her dying father with bright reminiscences of their days at Oxford. When the end did come, he had seen to it that his friend had a better funeral than Meriel could have provided. Lord Lithwaite had also attended to the selling of the cottage and its effects and though most of the money had gone to settle Sir Sylvian's debts, he had repeated to Meriel his earlier reassurances.

She had been so relieved and Lord Lithwaite had been uncommonly kind on their journey to London, seeing that she was given the best rooms at the inns where they were billeted. He had even bought her two black gowns, since she could not afford mourning attire. What might have been a most difficult and frightening period for her had been, through his tact and consideration, turned into a tolerably comfortable one.

Indeed, she had looked forward to her new life with excitement, actually imagining herself a member of the society she had only read about in the few periodicals that had found their way into her father's home. Then, she met Lady Lithwaite and Lord Algernon, the latter being nine in years and a hundred and nine when it came to the ingenuity with which he planned complicated and horrid surprises for his new governess. To think of Algernon was to again be happy that three hours intervened before she needed to enter the school room.

Meriel recalled how surprised she had been that a man as handsome and gracious as Lord Lithwaite had chosen to wed a plump little woman with round beady eyes, a pronounced double-chin, and an overbearing manner. She had been even more surprised by the boy his Lordship had indulgently described as "a bit high-spirited."

"A bit high-spirited!" Meriel mouthed. Her old nanny would not have hesitated to term him "a limb of Satan!" Yet, in a sense, it was not entirely his fault, for, as Lady Susan, his Lordship's daughter by his first marriage, had told her, the boy had been cosseted since birth.

"My stepmother has given strict orders that Algy never be slapped, spanked, or scolded. You must remember that." She had warned. "She has dismissed five governesses for chastising him."

At the thought of Lady Susan, Meriel's face softened. Susan was a lovely, blond girl of her own age, who favored her father in looks and in temperament as well. Meriel had liked her on sight, and it had been mutual.

"Oh, I am so glad you have come to stay with us," Lady Susan had told her, shortly after Meriel's arrival. "I've been very lonely here. Papa is away so often."

Meriel could understand that. The first Lady Lithwaite, a beautiful woman whose sweetness and charm were apparent even in the portrait that still graced the drawing room, had been killed in a hunting accident, leaving her husband desolate and without an heir. It had been solely for the sake of the title that he had married again. He had chosen his third cousin, who had reached the unfortunate age of twenty-nine without a single offer, even though possessed of a reasonably large dowry.

"After Mama died, Papa did not care whom he married, and my uncle suggested that she would be a good breeder." Lady Susan had flushed. "I do not expect he meant me to hear that."

"I imagine my papa would have married for much the same reasons had he been in Lord Lithwaite's position," Meriel had replied. "He never recovered his spirits after my mama died."

"Oh, we do have so much in common." Lady Susan had breathed. "We might be sisters, you know. I think we even look a little alike, except your hair is so very fair. It's really odd that your brows and lashes are dark."

"I expect it is," Meriel had answered vaguely. She had never really thought much about her looks. Her father, buried in his books, had never remarked upon them. However, whenever she had walked down the streets of Chalfont St. Giles, she had been aware of young men giving her long, disquieting stares, accompanied by rude but, by their standards, flattering remarks. Once, upon emerging from the County Records office, where she had gone to do research, she'd been accosted by a stranger, who had attempted to kiss her. She smiled gleefully, remembering his shock when she had expertly kicked him in the ankle before twisting out of his grasp and running away.

She'd been equally shocked, she recalled, by her own reaction. It had been spontaneous; and she had been so pleased by her inherent resourcefulness that she had confided the entire episode to her father. Meriel grimaced, remembering his reaction.

"Evidently," he had said, giving her a long cold look, "you were being deliberately provocative in your actions, else he would not have dared to approach a lady."

"P-provocative, Papa?" She had questioned, her slight stutter getting the best of her, as it always did when she was especially nervous.

"Walk across the room," he had ordered.

Wonderingly, she had obeyed and then, turning back had found a black frown on his forehead. "You are swinging your hips like any wanton." He had thundered. "Henceforth, you will endeavor to walk as ladies do. Take small steps and keep your back rigid. Now, walk for me, please." He had kept her walking up and down the chamber for an hour.

She sighed. "I should have known better." Her conscience told her. "I never ought to have confided in him." He had not welcomed her confidences nor had he evinced any interest in the life she lived outside of his library. To him, she had been only a convenience, someone to transcribe his notes and copy his manuscript. If she were truthful, Meriel could admit that she did not miss him at all. She had been prepared to be very happy at the home of Lord Lithwaite and, she thought, she could have been if only Lady Lithwaite had not disliked her on sight. Still, it might have been different had Lord Lithwaite remained at home. However, having deposited her at Lithwaite Mansion, he had departed the following morning. She shuddered a little as she recalled the interview she had had with Lady Lithwaite, immediately after his leave-taking.

"My husband has told me, Miss Hathaway, that you are an able instructress for the young. I find that difficult to believe, since he has also explained that this is your first position. However, I am willing to give you a trial.

"My husband has also suggested that you be included in the family circle. You will take your meals with us, but I find I cannot give you one of the chambers on the second floor, as they are being redecorated. I hope you'll not take it amiss that you reside on the fourth floor until such time as proper accommodations can be arranged. Unfortunately, these quarters are accessible only through the back of the house. I am sorry for the inconvenience, but I am sure you will understand.

"As for your duties. You will find that Lord Algernon has a fine mind and under the proper tutelage, he can be an excellent student. I look upon you to give him that tutelage and to inspire trust in him, which, I must add, cannot be done by force. Though I am aware that my viewpoint is not shared by the majority of parents, I am totally against corporal punishment. Lord Algernon has been raised in an atmosphere of love and kindness. I will not contenance any other form of treatment."

"Now, as to his daily schedule. You will teach him languages in the two hours before noon; history, geography, spelling, and mathematics in the afternoon. Your Thursday after-noons will be free."

Meriel had listened to Lady Lithwaite with a sinking heart. It had been only too clear to her that rather than being welcomed into the family circle, she was being inexorably thrust out of it, relegated to the position of an upper servant. Indeed, her chamber was one of six on the fourth floor; the other five being shared by several housemaids.

Lady Susan had been indignant at her stepmother's attitude. "I shall not fail to inform Papa when he comes home," she had declared.

"Please, please do not," Meriel had begged. "It will serve no purpose. He will be gone soon again, then she will be even more difficult."

"But he never intended you should be up-stairs like . . . like a servant," Lady Susan had cried. Actually, she did feel a little like a ser-vant, for though she was welcomed by Lady Susan and introduced to her friends, as soon as Lady Lithwaite came into the room, visitors were immediately made aware of Meriel's in-ferior status. The servants, too, treated her with a marked lack of respect, but the worst offender in that regard was Lord Algernon, who, being aware of his ascendency over her, seemed to take delight in tormenting her.

His persecution had started the day after her arrival. She remembered it as if it were yesterday, even though yesterday had had its own specific problems. Meriel had come into the school room, a large lovely chamber with a view of the gardens. There was a desk for her convenience, and the chair behind it, though straight of back, had a large cushion on it. Little Algernon also had a small desk, and he was seated behind it, when she entered. He was a handsome boy for, fortunately, he resembled his father, even though he had his mother's dark hair and brown eyes. These, rather than being small and piercing, were large and limpid. Indeed, he looked to be the very picture of innocent childhood. Meriel had smiled at him, and he had smiled back. Then, she'd taken her seat, only to rise immediately, for there had been a sharp pin in the cushion, so sharp that when she rose, the cushion stuck to her dress. The point of the pin had penetrated into her flesh.

Staring at her pupil, she had found him convulsed with laughter. "Did . . . you . . . do . . . this?" She had demanded, unnecessarily, since she knew full well that he had.

He had raised those big brown eyes to her. "No, Miss Hathaway, I should not do such a thing."

Her nails had dug into palms that were itching to spank him, but in her mind was Lady Lithwaite's firm injunction and Lord Lithwaite's kindness to her. She owed it to him to try and teach his son. Removing the cushion, she had resumed her seat. Calmly, she had said, "Very well, Lord Algernon, I shall take your word for it. Now, shall we begin our Latin lesson?"

She had read a certain disappointment in his eyes and it was at that moment that she'd been visited by an inspiration. He wanted to torment her, but she would refuse to be his victim. No matter what he did, she would remain bland and noncommittal. It might not halt his persecution, but certainly it would take some of the joy out of it, as far as he was concerned. It had. It most certainly had.

She sighed, remembering snails and slugs in her desk drawer and a little green garter snake, as well. She had coolly dropped them out of the window into the garden. Then, there had been the pail of water that had drenched her one morning after she had opened the school-room door; it had taken a real effort to refrain from shaking him until his teeth rattled, but she had only excused herself and gone up to her chamber to change her gown and dry her hair, coming down to face him as calmly as though nothing out of the way had taken place, as if, indeed, a jug of water on her head was part of her everyday experience.

She had been equally noncommittal when he had spread glue on the back of her chair, necessitating that her dress be cut off of it. Since she had so few garments, Lady Lithwaite had grudgingly given her the money to purchase material for a new gown, which had been run up by the lady's own seamstress. However, nothing was said in criticism of her son. "He is only high-spirited, you understand." She had insisted, her eyes fixed on Meriel's face, as if daring her to contradict.

Thinking about Lady Lithwaite, Meriel knew the woman disliked her heartily and enjoyed tormenting her. Yet, surprisingly enough, she was not totally unhappy and that, she realized, was due to her friendship with Lady Susan.

Lady Susan had proved to be a true

friend. She was kind and gentle. She always made an effort to include Meriel in her social activities; she went walking with her in the park or accompanied her to the lending library on her free Thursdays. On the evenings she spent at home, she saw that Meriel remained with her in the music room or the library. She had also confided in her that Lady Lithwaite had no more love for her step-daughter than for herself. "She is jealous of me because I am Papa's daughter and she is jealous of you because Papa brought you here and because you are so pretty."

"I am not pretty," Meriel had told her.

"How can you say that?" Lady Susan had marveled. "You have that lovely hair and your eyes are so very blue . . ."

"As are yours," Meriel had replied.

"Mine are pale blue, but yours are dark like . . . like deep forest pools. That's a description I read in a novel, but it fits."

"I should think that deep forest pools would be either black or a muddy green." Meriel had laughed.

"Very well—like violets." Lady Susan had joined in her laughter, but then she had sobered. "I do wish you were my sister, for then she'd dare not treat you so scurvily. The Lady cannot be unkind to me, no matter how she would like to be, for she once was and Papa heard of it. Probably one of the servants told him, for they were here in Mama's time and though she wanted to dismiss them and hire new ones, Papa would not countenance it. They are all very fond of me. At any rate, he took Step-Mama into the library and remained closeted with her for an hour. After that, she never opened her mouth in anger to me again. I know she looks forward to the day when I shall be wed to Norbert."

Norbert was Major Norbert Campion, currently fighting with his regiment in America, but they had recently heard that he had been wounded during the campaign in the capital and was being invalided home. "It's his leg." Lady Susan had told Meriel. "He was shot twice, but he'll not lose it and he may not have to return to his regiment." A trifle defiantly, she had added, "I am glad that he was hurt, otherwise he might have been killed. I do hate war! It is all so useless."

Meriel had agreed with her. She, too, was pleased at Major Campion's return, but she did not look forward to a time when she would be left alone without the leavening presence of her friend. Truly, Lady Susan was most understanding.

"I really do not see how you manage to put up with Algy," she had said on more than one occasion. "He is such a bad little boy."

"I am in hopes that one day he will tire of his pranks," Meriel had replied.

"Perhaps . . ." Lady Susan had sounded doubtful.

Meriel was also doubtful. She sighed and shook her head.

"Ah, what have we here?" a voice spoke in her ear. Startled out of her musing, she blinked up to find herself facing a tall, elderly man in evening attire. He had a narrow face, dominated by hooded, gray eyes that were bloodshot and set in deep pouches. There was a look in them that repelled her. Even less engaging was the smile that played about his over-full mouth.

Instinctively, she stepped backward only to have him catch her arm and hold it in a hard grip. "I must ask you to let me go, Sir," she said, indignantly, while trying to pull away from him.

His grip tightened. "Why should I do that?" he drawled. "Surely, you've been walking these pavements looking for such a one as I? Are you fearful, I've not the price of . . . admission? I assure you, I've had a most successful evening at the tables and now . . . the morning dawns even brighter in my eyes."

He drew her close to him, so close she could smell his brandy-scented breath. Pushing back her bonnet, he stared down into her frightened face. "By God!" He smiled, exposing ugly yellowed teeth. "You're as pretty a bit o'muslin as I've seen of late. Indeed, its a wonder some gallant's not set you up in Chelsea—a lovely face and a shape to match. I'll warrant you'll give me rare sport, 'ere we're done."

Meriel raised both hands and pushed against him. "Let me go," she cried again, not understanding the import of his words, but more frightened than she had ever been in her whole life. There was something horrid in the hardness of his stare. Then, to her utter revulsion, he ran the tip of a pale, pointed tongue around his lips. Feeling almost physically ill, she panted. "I pray you, let me go." She made another effort to break free from him.

"I shall let you go, my pretty." He smiled

darkly. "I live not two steps from here, and once we're inside, you shall have the . . . er run of my house." Clamping an arm around her shoulders, he urged her toward the street.

"No, no, no," Meriel gasped. "I do not want to g-go to your house. I will n-not!" She tried to stiffen her small body against his hard arm, but to no avail. He was surprisingly strong for a man of his years, which she reckoned to be at least fifty!

"I tell you, I have your price, my dear. I shall fill your . . . slipper with gold." His laughter, low and insinuating made her shudder. Frantically, she looked about her and seeing a man approaching, she called, "Sir . . . sir, I beg you help me. I . . ." but the man passed by, unseeing and unhearing. Indeed, no one on the street seemed interested in her plight.

"Please . . . let me go!"

"Come," her captor suddenly snarled. "Enough of this play-acting. Do you think to raise your price?"

Suddenly, there was the clatter of horses' hooves and the rattle of an equipage. Out of the corner of her eye, Meriel saw a curricle coming down the street. Making another effort to free herself, she screamed loudly, "Help, help, please! Help me, help . . ." Only to receive a stinging slap across the face from her captor.

"I said, that's enough, girl."

Vaguely, she heard the horses being pulled to a stop; then someone was hurrying across the cobblestone street.

"Miss Hathaway!"

Meriel, her eyes filled with tears of fright and pain from the blow, blinked up at a tall, handsome young man, also in evening attire. To her great relief, she recognized him as Lord Neville Farr, Earl of Farringdon and Lord Lithwaite's nephew. "Oh, p-please, my L-Lord," she sobbed. "This m-man . . . he . . . he . . ."

Summing up the situation immediately, the Earl said angrily, "Release her! How dare you force your attentions on this young lady?"

Drawing himself up haughtily, the older man answered coldly, "I cannot see where it concerns you. I am quite willing to pay her price . . ."

"Her price!" echoed the Earl. "You must be foxed, else you'd see she's a gently-bred young woman who . . ."

"Who has been walking the streets unescorted," the other finished coldly. "I'll have you know that I am Lord Hove and I do not take insults lightly."

"Do you not, my Lord?" the Earl's flashing smile was mocking. "Would you be suggesting I name my seconds?"

"Oh, no, please!" Meriel gasped.

Lord Hove's eyes dwelt on Meriel for a second longer. There was an ugly expression in them, and his mouth curled into a sneer. "I think not, my Lord," he said softly. "Unlike you, I am not so quick to fight over . . . strumpets." Wheeling away from them, he quickly crossed the street, disappearing through the portals of a large mansion.

"Strumpets, is it?" The Earl frowned. "I've a good mind to . . ." He made a move in the direction taken by Lord Hove.

"No, I pray you'll do nothing, my Lord

Farr." Meriel put her hand on his arm. "I expect it was all my fault. I should not have been walking by myself."

He stared down at her. Lord Farr was known as a prankster and, generally, there was a smile on his face and a mischievous look in his large brown eyes, but neither expression was visible at the moment. He said gravely, "No, indeed, you should not. Why are you here, Miss Hathaway, so early in the morning and such a great distance from my uncle's house?"

"A . . . great distance?" Meriel faltered. "I'm but a step away . . ." She stared around her and paled, not recognizing any of the houses or anything else about the street. "It . . . it was such a lovely day. I thought to go for a short walk, but I was deep in thought and I did not see where I was going. I'd no notion I'd come so far." Helplessly, she added, "I do not know where I am."

"You are on Charles Street," Lord Farr told her, shaking his head. "It must have been providence that brought me here, else I should hate to think what might have happened to you. London is not Chalfont St. Giles, Miss Hathaway."

"I know." Meriel looked at him gratefully. "I have not thanked you for saving me from that horrid man."

"I am only glad I was here." He shook his head. "But you must promise me, you'll not put yourself in such jeopardy again. You should never go walking without an abigail to attend you."

"An abigail for a governess?" she inquired wryly.

"Given your background and breeding, I do not see . . ." He began, then frowning, he said, "No matter, I shall drive you home, or, rather, I shall set you down within a moment's walk of your home. I think we need not acquaint my aunt with an account of your morning's adventure."

"No, please, we must not," she cried, her eyes round with worry.

"Come then." He escorted her to his curricle. "I shall be waiting on my cousin later this morning." He winked at her. "Then, should we meet, we will be discreet."

She laughed. "I doubt that we shall meet, my Lord, for I shall be closeted with Lord Algernon."

The Earl winced.

It was odd, Meriel thought, as she combed her hair at the small mirror set above the bench that served as dressing table in her cramped little room, she had passed one of the most perilous mornings of her life and, yet, she could not dwell on the danger that had threatened her. She could only take delight in the fact that she had been with Lord Farr, and had ridden in his curricle behind his famous matched grays. She had only the most fleeting memory of their noble heads and flowing manes. Mostly, she had limited herself to directing surreptitious side-glances at Neville Farr's sun-browned face and waving chestnut hair, as he expertly tooled his horses along the street. Truly, he was one of the most elegant and handsome young men she had ever seen. Also, one of the kindest, she thought, for unlike many of Lady Susan's friends, he had never let her feel that because of her poverty, she was any less deserving of his courtesy and respect.

She flushed, contrasting his attitude with that of Miss Beatrix Stansfield, known to the Carleton House set as an "Incomparable." Miss Stansfield was not only a friend of Lady Susan, she was the great love of Lord Neville Farr. Meriel had glimpsed her often from a distance, but she had met her only once, on a rainy Thursday afternoon some six weeks earlier, when she had been with Lady Susan in the music room.

Meriel had been unprepared for the vision that had swept into the chamber. She could still picture Beatrix in her stylish, brown walking dress, which showed off a slender figure to perfection. Her hair, rain-coaxed into springing curls to frame her oval face, was a ravishing shade of russet; and her eyes were blue-green or green-blue—Meriel was not sure which—with long, dark curling lashes. The Incomparable Beatrix's nose was straight, her brows delicately arched, while her mouth—here Meriel mentally paused. Though she knew from Lady Susan that Lord Farr had rather unoriginally compared Miss Stansfield's mouth to "a half-opened rosebud," she, Meriel, could not be so flattering. The feature in question was small for the rest of her face, and Miss Stansfield had a habit of compressing her lips, which made her look disapproving even when she had not intended it. However, Meriel had the definite feeling that Miss Stansfield had disapproved of her. Her haughtiness had been unmistakable when Meriel had been presented. Of course, Beatrix had asked the inevitable question: "Hathaway . . . er, would you be any relation to . . . Anne? Was it not?"

"No. I cannot claim kinship with the Bard of Avon," Meriel had replied with a smile.

"Oh, really not?" Miss Stansfield directed those words at her without interest.

Meriel excused herself within a few minutes of the Incomparable's arrival. Since it was her custom to be absolutely honest with herself in the hours that preceded her sessions with Lord Algernon, she now whispered, "I do not like Miss Stansfield."

"Yes, but Lord Farr does," averred her Other Self.

"What does that matter?" Meriel demanded indignantly.

"He'll not have much joy of her." She tittered a trifle cruelly.

"I am told he is quite a creditable magician." Meriel mused. "I wonder . . ."

"You wonder," said her irrepressible Other Self, "what she would do if he were to remove an egg from her décolletage, as he did from that of Lady Agatha Moreley at the Prince's reception last Tuesday. Lady Susan said that the *on dit* is that Lady Agatha's husband nearly called him out for it. I do not think Miss Stansfield would approve, either. Lady Susan has said that she deplores his magic tricks. She would. She has no sense of humor."

"You must stop talking about Lord Farr." Meriel addressed her obtrusive Other Self sharply.

"And you," cautioned that Self, "must stop

26

thinking about him, if I am to stop talking about him."

"I will, then," Meriel said defiantly. But it was impossible not to conjure up yet another picture of him in her mind's eye, to dwell on the length of eyelashes, which exceeded even those of Miss Stansfield's. That morning, Meriel had noticed that his, too, curled at the ends. Of course, they were not artificially darkened as she believed Miss Stansfield's to be. She particularly liked his mouth. It was not too wide and not too narrow, but firm, showing strength. There was strength in his square chin, too, and she'd always admired a cleft. He dressed beautifully, in the height of fashion; his clothes fitting as well as Brummell's, at least that is what Lady Susan told her. Meriel never had had the opportunity of seeing the famous Beau. Even this morning, when Lord Farr had obviously been out all the night, his suit had fitted with not a wrinkle, and his linen had been as snowy as if he had just donned it. "Oh!" She groaned out loud. "Why, why am I running on like this. He has never really noticed me at all!"

"Not true," contradicted Other Self, now reduced to a still, small voice. "He said you had very unusual hair, like spun silk; and he remarked on its color, too."

"As did Lady Lithwaite." Meriel reminded that Self with a twisted smile. "She said my hair was so pale, I was fortunate I did not have pink eyes like a white mouse."

She frowned, still angry over Lady Lithwaite's cruel words. Yet, she was not the first to comment so. Many people had been surprised

27

by hair of so pale a gold. Meriel could not imagine how she'd come by it, but her father had advanced a theory. "The Scandinavians often have hair that shade." He had told her. "It is possible that one of our remote ancestors was a marauding Dane or Norwegian."

It was a romantic explanation, she had always thought. She could imagine a tall, brawny, pale-haired Viking, stepping out of his long-boat and striding across Britain's sands, to seize some hapless Saxon maiden in his arms. Probably, he would have tossed her over his shoulder and . . . Meriel blinked, finding that she was staring into the bright sunlight, reflected in her mirror, a sun already high in the sky. With a little gasp, she glanced down at the lapel watch, which had been one of her father's few presents to her. Its tiny hands pointed to half-past nine!

"What have I been thinking about?" Meriel exclaimed, as she jumped up and started for the door.

"Nothing constructive," commented Self-Two dryly.

# (2)

At ten, Meriel came down the long hallway toward the school room. She approached it with even more reluctance than usual. She always needed at least half an hour of silent communion with her soul to strengthen herself for the ordeal of Lord Algernon. She had not had it this morning. As always, upon reaching the door, she opened it cautiously, standing back and pushing it wider with her foot. Thus, if there was a pitcher of water rigged to drench her, it would only wet the floor. However, the door swung back easily, and when she went into the sunny school room, it was to find that Lord Algernon had not yet arrived. That was odd, for it was a few moments past the hour and, generally, he was very prompt.

Meriel cast a speculative eye around the

room, wondering if he was lingering in a corner, waiting to pop out at her. He had done that more than once and been sadly disappointed when she'd neither jumped nor screamed. Indeed, in the past two weeks, she could pride herself that nothing Lord Algernon had done had appeared to startle her, not even yesterday when on opening her desk drawer, she had found it full of pastry flour. She'd said with her usual calm, "I do believe, Lord Algernon, that your ingenuity is faltering. Soon you'll not be able to think of anything either new or startling enough to confound me."

He had given her a baleful glare before settling down to his Latin verbs, but had refrained from comment. It was possible, Meriel thought, that he was on the verge of ending his program of surprise attacks. She hoped so, because, if she had not had to be on her guard each morning, there might have been some pleasure in instructing him. He was a bright boy. He had a quick grasp of most subjects, as well as an inquiring and original turn of mind. If only he was not aware that he was Lord and Master in the house. She wished that she had the courage to write to Lord Lithwaite to beg him to spend more time with his son.

She looked around for Lord Algernon again. Perhaps he was ill. Her eyes gleamed and a little smile curled the corners of her mouth. She quelled it quickly. It was wrong to wish sickness on anyone, even the Lithwaite heir. She opened her desk drawer, cautiously again, but it was as neatly arranged as it had been the previous day, after she'd managed to shake all the flour out of it. Taking out her Latin grammar, a pad of paper, and a pencil, Meriel opened the book, preparing to write down some questions. She was engaged in this pursuit when she felt a current of air go through the room. The door had been opened. Stifling a sigh, she said without turning, "Good morning, Lord Algernon."

There was no response. Surprised, she cast a glance in the direction of the door. It was closed, and she did not see Lord Algernon. Perhaps he had opened it and closed it. Perhaps he was lurking in the hall, expecting her to come out and see why he had not entered. Suddenly, she was on the alert and positive that something was about to happen.

The quiet that prevailed in the room had become ominous rather than reassuring. It was the calm before the storm. What could he be planning? She was most certainly not going to go into the hall to find out. She forced herself to concentrate on her Latin grammar and started writing out the sentences she wanted him to translate. Suddenly, she felt moisture falling rapidly on her head from above, seeping through her hair and dribbling down her left cheek. With a little cry that she could not suppress, Meriel put her hand up to her cheek. On taking it down, she screamed—for her palm had turned blue!

"Blue, blue, you're all blue!" Lord Algernon chortled gleefully, as he jumped around the side of the desk, grinning from ear to ear.

Dazed, she looked at him. He was blue, too. Her gaze fell on his little hands and she saw he was carrying the great silver and crystal inkwell from the library desk. *"Ink!"* she shrieked and clapped a hand to her head. It was very wet, and when she looked at her palm a second time, she found it to be even bluer. Leaping to her feet, Meriel launched herself at Lord Algernon and slapped him sharply on both sides of his face. "You little devil," she cried, shaking him. "You . . ."

He wrenched himself out of her frenzied grasp and for a split second, was silent. Then, with a great howl of rage, he ran screaming from the room.

A pouter pigeon.

The thought drifted through Meriel's dazed mind when, three hours later, she stood in the school room looking at Lady Lithwaite. She'd never noticed it before, but her soon-to-be-former employer did resemble the bird in question. All her weight seemed pushed up into her chest and, indeed, she was swelling up just like a pouter pigeon. Her emotion was all too discernible in her figure-revealing gown. The styles of 1815, while fuller than those of 1803, were still not flattering to pigeons. She had pigeon eyes, too, Meriel mused—black and beady. Pigeon eyes, pigeon chest, and a pigeon brain, for how could any woman in her right mind blame her for having slapped Lord Algernon. But that was precisely what Lady Lithwaite was doing.

"Imagine," she said, and not for the first time. "Striking my poor little angelic Algernon, my darling baby boy—and after I told you what I thought about corporal punishment. Do you realize, Miss Hathaway, that never, *never* in all of his nine years has a hand been raised to him in anger or cruelty?"

Meriel, remembering Lady Susan's reference to his five previous governesses, still refrained from comment. She had already given her side of the matter; actually, it was not necessary to give it, for it was quite evident. Her hair was blue. The top of her head was all blue, but the right side was mostly blond—it was the left that had received the greater portion of the dribbling ink, nor had it grown any fainter with the several soapings she had given it.

"It is . . . unfortunate about your hair." Lady Lithwaite allowed. "But you should have taken his extreme youth into consideration. He is a trifle mischievous as are all other children at his age." She paused and swelled again. "Slapping him on his poor little face; it was such a shock to his sensibilities. He'd grown to trust you, Miss Hathaway, and now—to have that trust destroyed . . . I only hope it will not have a deleterious effect upon his character."

"I hope not, Lady Lithwaite," Meriel said, striving to keep a sarcastic inflection from her voice.

"If that is by way of being an apology," Lady Lithwaite said, "it will not change my mind. As I have told you, I expect you to be out of this house by tomorrow morning. I will give you your next quarter's wages, which, under the circumstances, I consider most generous. I will not, however, be able to provide you with a reference. Contrary to my husband's beliefs, I do not think you possess the proper temperament for instructing the young." There was a look in the black beady eyes which Meriel could interpret all too easily. In dismissing her, Lady Lithwaite was not only ridding herself of a young woman whose presence she had resented from the first, she was revenging herself on the husband who, once he was provided with the requisite heir, had faded almost completely from her life.

If she had not deserved the treatment he had accorded her, Meriel thought, one could almost feel sorry for Lady Lithwaite. Thus, it was less difficult for her to swallow the retort she would have preferred to hurl at her ex-employer. Meriel answered softly, "I quite understand, Milady."

"I hope that this will be a lesson you'll not soon forget," Lady Lithwaite snapped.

Since the lesson was couched in indelible blue ink, Meriel could say truthfully, "No, I am sure I shall not, Milady."

"Very well," Lady Lithwaite said grandly. "You may go. Your supper will be served in your room. Afterward, I suggest you pack. Tomorrow morning, I shall have my coachman drive you to other lodgings. I have asked my housekeeper to prepare a list of inexpensive but safe hostels for young women in your situation. Please be ready at ten."

"Yes, Milady." Meriel dropped a curtsey and went out of the school room, and through the hall to the back stairs. In a sense, the back stairs reminded her of Lady Lithwaite. They were narrow, creaking, and with only the light from a window on the floor above illuminating them. They were also sunk in gloom.

Setting her foot upon the first step, Meriel whispered, "She has a narrow, creaking, gloomy soul." She heaved a sigh. Castigating her former employer might cheer her briefly, but it did nothing to change matters. It was fortunate for Lady Lithwaite that her Lord was in the country. If he had been in residence, she was sure that he never would have countenanced so arbitrary an action. But Meriel could not think of that. Lord Lithwaite was in the country, and she was all alone with nowhere to turn. Earlier, Lady Susan had wept and pressed a few pounds into Meriel's unwilling hand. "You must take it." Lady Susan had insisted. "I would I had more, and you may be sure that if Papa comes home in the next day or so . . ."

The two girls had looked at each other hopelessly. The prospect of Lord Lithwaite's return was highly unlikely, and while Meriel could afford to remain in a lodging house for, perhaps, a fortnight, she had no idea what she would do once her money ran out. No one would hire a governess without references. Of course, she could hire herself out as a housemaid or even work in the scullery. She shuddered. Neither prospect seemed enticing, and, then, there was her hair! How could she work anywhere with blue hair? Even if she were to cut it off, the stain would remain on the part that was left. She touched her assaulted head and sighed, wistfully wishing that she could have taken a strong strap to Lord Algernon's backside. She could not dwell on that; it was not the cause but the effect which need concern her now and . . . and . . . She sighed again.

Then, resolutely, she firmed her mouth. She would not think about her miserable situation, not yet. It was all confusing. She needed to rest, first.

She toiled on up the stairs and had nearly reached the second floor when she heard her name called.

Startled by the sound of a voice that she recognized immediately, Meriel clutched the balustrade quickly and, turning, found herself staring down into Lord Farr's face. "My . . . my L-Lord," she said faintly. "W-what are you . . . doing back here?"

He gave her a commiserating glance. "My poor Miss Hathaway," he said, ruefully. "Surely the Fates have treated you most unkindly today. Lady Susan has told me what has happened." He hurried up to her. "Lord, Lord!" He frowned. "These stairs are steep and dark, too. I'd no idea it was so dismal in this part of the house. I shouldn't be surprised if there were black beetles skulking about beneath our toes."

"There are certainly beetles," she agreed. "They are black and very large, but I do not mind them."

"No, undoubtedly, you prefer them to Algeron. I should."

In spite of her distress, she had to laugh. "I most certainly do."

"I should have done much more than merely slapping him." Lord Farr frowned.

"So should I have," she said, frankly. "But the circumstances were against it."

He raised his eyebrows. "I vow, I do admire your spirit, Miss Hathaway. You are very calm in the face of adversity."

She looked down quickly. "I . . . I fear you exaggerate, my Lord, for sure I was not very calm this morning."

"I disagree. Any other female would have treated me to a full-fledged case of the vapors, but you did not. For that I give you my hearty congratulations." He paused, then, a little diffidently, he continued. "I cannot see your hair in this Stygian darkness, but there's a window up higher. Might you go up there and let me see it?"

She tensed. "Why would you want to see my hair, my Lord?" she asked, adding more bitterly than she intended, "I expect you'd find it amusing, given what your cousin describes as your 'notable sense of humor.' Rather than looking like spun silk, I fear you'll find it now resembles embroidery silk: blue."

The moment she had unleashed those words, she regretted them. She was especially sorry that she let him know she remembered his little compliment. Inadvertently, she'd given it an importance it ought not to have warranted.

Much to her relief, his answer revealed that he had not noticed the reference. "No, Miss Hathaway," he replied earnestly. "I do not think it in the least amusing, or I shouldn't if I were you," he concluded ingenuously. "Lady Susan tells me that it will not come out."

"No, it won't," she snapped.

"I must see it," he cried, eagerly.

His attitude did not please her. She suspected him of wanting to laugh at her, or, if not that, of a morbid curiosity which was equally unlikable. Momentarily forgetting his kindness of the morning, she drew herself up, and said, coldly, "My Lord Farr, I find your request highly unusual and I also find it very strange to see you in this part of the house. If Lady Lithwaite knew you were here, I am sure she would be extremely annoyed."

His dark eyes were full of unabashed laughter. "Come, come, we both know she would be furious. She is usually furious, but that should not matter to either of us, Miss Hathaway. Neither of us is in her employ, and I assure you, I have a most particular reason to see your hair—one that might prove of great benefit to us both."

"B-B-Benefit?" she stammered, incredulously.

"Will you come?" Masterfully, he put his hand under her arm, propelling her up the next few steps to the second floor, and sending tendrils of excitement up her arm. "Ah," he said, sighting the window at the end of the hall. "Come, Miss Hathaway."

Too bemused to argue, she let him lead her to it, but once they were there, she wanted to run and hide rather than see the smile her hair must provoke from him. Defensively, she raised both hands to her head only to have him pull them down, while he examined her locks closely.

Finally, and without a trace of laughter, he said, "The little beast. I wish I might have had the punishing of Lord Algernon, my poor Miss Hathaway. Believe me, my uncle shall hear of the episode from me. However, all is not lost. It is a condition which can, as I have hoped, be turned to your advantage and mine. I can only pray that you will agree—though I know you will think my request unusual, at the very least."

"My advantage and . . . yours?" Meriel repeated, selecting the sentence from his speech that had interested her the most. "What manner of request had you in mind, my Lord?"

"None," he said seriously. "At least not in the usual sense of the word. Your blue hair has inspired me. Indeed, it is all so fortuitous that I cannot help but feel it was Fate's hand guided that ink bottle."

"Fate?" she repeated, bewildered. "What can you mean?"

For the first time, there was a gleam of amusement in Lord Farr's eyes. "It will take a certain amount of explaining, Miss Hathaway, and I've no wish to do it in the middle of the hall." His lip curled. "Is there somewhere in this . . . rabbit warren, where we might be private?"

In spite of his denials, Meriel was still convinced that he was planning one of the elaborate practical jokes for which he was famous among his cronies. It was on the tip of her tongue to tell him she wanted no part of it, but on the other hand, her curiosity was aroused. Besides, if she were to dismiss him now, there was every chance that she might never see him again. She found that thought singularly depressing. Looking around her, she said, "I . . . do not know . . . Perhaps . . ."

"A linen closet? An attic?" he prompted.

"An attic!" she exclaimed. "Yes, there is an attic, but . . ."

"Where is it?" he asked excitedly, his dark eyes gleaming.

"It's on the fourth floor. Lord Algernon took me there one rainy afternoon, shortly after I arrived."

"Good," Lord Farr interrupted. "Then you may show it to me."

Meriel looked at him doubtfully. "But, my Lord . . ." she began nervously, "it does not seem right that I . . . that we . . ."

"Are you concerned about the propriety of the situation, Miss Hathaway?" he asked with the hint of a chuckle.

She could not meet his eyes. "Well . . . I . . ."

"My dear Miss Hathaway." He smiled. "I can assure you that if you were my own sister, I could not respect you more. You will be quite safe with me—far safer than you were wandering the London streets in the early morning hours."

She blushed. "I . . . I know . . . I did but think . . ."

"I hope that I can give you something far more constructive to dwell upon than the possible loss of your virtue." He paused, adding, "Do any of the servants visit this attic at odd moments?"

"I do not believe so, my Lord. Hardly anyone goes there."

"Then, avaunt!" he said gaily. "Lead on Macduff."

She had to smile. "Follow me, my Lord." Meriel led him back to the stairs, and as they mounted them, she had a curious sense of having made a momentous decision, one which would have a far-reaching effect on her entire life. Much as she endeavored to persuade herself that this was pure nonsense, the conviction grew with each step she took.

The door to the attic was so small that even she had to stoop as she went inside.

"By all that's Holy," Lord Farr exclaimed as he followed her into an immense but low-ceilinged chamber. "What a clutter!"

The light from a pair of small dormer windows revealed an amazing conglomeration. Furniture of all styles from the early eighteenth century to the present was heaped together. There were great trunks. Some, due to Lord Algernon's insatiable curiosity, gaped open revealing discarded ball gowns and dusty, powdered wigs. In a far corner, a collection of beakers and a rusting cauldron indicated a possible interest in chemistry on the part of some former Lithwaite. There was also a broken spinning wheel and near it, a stack of family portraits in chipped gilt frames. Stacks of battered books were piled against the side wall, and nearby was a pile of moldering newspapers. Heaps of what appeared to be draperies or possibly bed-hangings overlapped each other on the floor, making walking difficult if not hazardous.

A certain painful memory caused Meriel to exclaim hastily, "Keep your head down, my Lord!"

She was a split second too late with her warning, as he grazed his head on a beam. "Damnit," he muttered, adding quickly, "I beg your pardon, Miss Hathaway."

"I hope you did not hurt yourself," she said, anxiously.

"There are those who'd have it my head's the hardest part of my anatomy," he told her solemnly.

She could not repress a giggle. Then, on taking another step, she stumbled over a fallen candlestick and would have gone down had he not caught her adroitly, holding her against his chest for an enthralling moment. "Come, we must find a place to sit, else we'll both be much the worse for this adventure."

"Thank you for . . . for saving me from a bad fall," she said a little breathlessly, knowing she was blushing again and hoping that the semi-darkness of the chamber might prevent him seeing her bright cheeks. She added quickly, "Here, this might do." She indicated a long graceful settee, covered in green-gold velvet.

"Yes, it might." He looked at it closely, running a hand along its cushion. "I remember this, I always thought it very beautiful. If I am not mistaken it used to be in the drawing room. I wonder why it was brought up here. It seems in good condition."

"I expect it did not fit in with the new Egyptian decor," Meriel speculated.

"Egyptian!" Lord Farr snorted. "By no stretch of the imagination could one call the furniture she has assembled in her drawing room Egyptian! It is an abomination, and quite in line with the other changes she has wrought. What a fool my uncle was to wed her. With his own two hands he cast all happiness away. One should never marry unless it is for love, I am convinced of that, no matter what our match-making, dowry-conscious elders might say to the contrary. Do you not agree, Miss Hathaway?"

"I-I've not thought about it overmuch, but I expect it would be better to be wed to someone you loved," Meriel agreed, as she sat down on one end of the settee.

Sitting himself at the other end, Lord Farr said, "It's very musty in here."

"Musty and cobwebby." She nodded. "We'd best not inhale this air for very long." A little self-consciously, she added, "I do not think I should have brought you here."

"We'll not stay long," he promised. "But you must listen to me, Miss Hathaway. As you have doubtlessly been informed by my cousin, I am in love."

"Miss Stansfield." Meriel nodded.

"Yes," he sighed. "With the beautiful, incomparable Miss Stansfield, who is currently in the throes of deciding whether she will favor my suit or that of my Cousin Rex, blast him, who also happens to be the Eleventh Duke of Broxbridge." Anger gleamed in his eyes. "It is entirely due to my own folly that they met! If I'd had the sense to hold my tongue, if I'd not praised her charms so highly when I went shooting with him on his estates in Yorkshire, he'd not have posted up to town to meet her. But what is the use of dwelling on the past? They met, and he was immediately smitten by her beauty. He began to shower her with attentions, and when I taxed him with the fact that I loved her, indeed that I worshipped the ground upon which she set her little foot, his only answer was the highly unoriginal: 'May the best man win, Neville.'

"However, in my estimation, he has taken an unfair advantage of me by inviting Miss Stansfield and her ambitious parent, Lady Stansfield, to visit him at Broxbridge Hall. Obviously, he believes that a dukedom is a vastly superior incentive to matrimony than a mere earldom. Furthermore, there is his ancient castle and broad acreage, all of which must impress Lady Stansfield. I am sure that that grasping old harridan will most certainly endeavor to persuade her daughter to accept my cousin's offer, no matter what Miss Stansfield's own inclinations may be." He sighed. "I might add that in the past, she did not show herself indifferent to me."

Meriel gave him an incredulous look. She had never seen the Duke, but in her estimation neither land nor title could have turned her mind from the attractions of Lord Farr. She said gently, "I cannot think that Miss Stansfield will be moved to agree with her mother."

"You are most kind, Miss Hathaway, and it is not that I doubt the depth of Miss Stansfield's feelings for me, but she is also devoted to her mother and surely she, too, cannot help but be impressed by what she will find at the Hall. However"—a twinkle flickered briefly in his eyes—"there is one serious drawback. Miss Stansfield is a young lady of great sensibility. Furthermore, she possesses a most lively imagination. I know that from my cousin, who tells me that she once loaned her a novel by some female who writes of haunted castles, peopled by headless specters and shrieking beldams. Miss Stansfield was so affected by this gloomy tale that she was unable to sleep for three

44

nights running, for fear the doors and windows of her chamber would soon be creaking open to reveal walking skeletons and hovering shades."

"Gracious," Meriel marveled. "Can she actually believe in such things?"

He cocked an interested eye at her. "Don't you?"

"Certainly not!" Meriel exclaimed tartly.

"Ah," he said eagerly. "All the better."

"Why?"

He leaned forward, looking at her earnestly. "Listen to me, Miss Hathaway. I think I might be able to discourage the Duke's pursuit of the Incomparable by causing a legend to come to life."

"A legend?"

"Yes, may I tell it to you?"

"Please."

"Some four hundred years ago, a certain Lord Wynthorpe, the family name of the Broxbridges, as you might know, fell in love with a beautiful village maiden. I believe she was the daughter of the local blacksmith. Being a good honest, virtuous girl, she tried to repulse his advances, but he had his way with her and they became lovers.

"Then, one day he was out riding in the forest and he happened to meet the Lady Ursula Broadlands, the daughter of the neighboring baron. He was smitten by her beauty and he completely forgot the blacksmith's daughter.

"Hearing of his impending nuptials, the unfortunate young woman came to the castle to beg his help, since she was expecting a child.

Infuriated, he took her up to the North Turret of his castle and flung her into the moat. However, as he was pushing her from the tower, she cursed him, saying that the Broxbridges would always die before their time and that she would arrive to warn each heir of his inescapable doom. As she foretold, so it happened. Not long after the Duke married his Ursula, a dripping maiden appeared on the North Turret, crying, 'Doom, Doom, Doom to the Broxbridges!' He was subsequently killed by a wild boar in the forest. The next heir, his son, also died young in battle, and again, servants and kindred saw and heard the dripping maiden. She is known, I might add, as the Blue Lady of Broxbridge Hall or, more colloquially as 'Lady Blue'. Though it has been several generations since she last appeared, the legend still survives."

There was a brief silence in the room, as Meriel regarded Lord Farr a trifle suspiciously. "You say she is known as 'Lady Blue'? Why would that be, my Lord?"

Meeting her eyes, he smiled. "I think you must have guessed the reason, Miss Hathaway —because for some supernatural reason, which no one can explain, she is all blue: skin, hair, eyes and gown."

Meriel drew a long breath. "I see. In other words, you want me to haunt the North Turret and scare Miss Stansfield into refusing the Duke."

Lord Farr's eyes brightened. "I can only applaud your perspicacity, Miss Hathaway." Eager, yet pleading he continued. "It would be for only one night, just long enough for the

46

servants to take fright and spread the news through the courtyard—from whence the North Turret is visible. I know it sounds like a ridiculous scheme, but first let me mention that Miss Stansfield is aware of the legend and has asked Lady Susan if she believes in it. I think my cousin has discouraged her upon the matter. Yet, if the specter actually appears, I feel she would be less inclined to favor Rex's suit, especially since he has a great fondness for Broxbridge Hall and is in residence there a good part of the year. I might add that if you would agree to help me, you would be well-paid, and I would see that you were comfortably situated."

"You would pay me?" Meriel asked.

"Of course," he looked surprised. "You cannot imagine that I should ask you to perform such a service out of mere kindness. I should not only pay you well, I should . . . indeed, I will find you a position. My old governess, Miss Selina Chance, keeps a school in Bath. I will recommend you as a teacher—" He hesitated, looking at her apologetically. "I am quite aware that I should be commending you to her at once, but it will take some time for your hair to grow out and it would be most helpful if you would consent to aid me."

Though the scheme he had described was certainly bizarre, Meriel realized that it definitely was not one of his practical jokes. There was not even the suspicion of a twinkle in his eyes. On the contrary, he looked wistful, even a little sad. Abiding the policy that all is fair in love and war, he was eager to try anything in order to win the indecisive Incom-

47

parable. This in spite of a certain fickleness of nature that another less infatuated man might notice. Spurred on by the memory of his kindness that morning, Meriel asked, cautiously, "How is it possible to get into the castle?"

"You mean that you . . . might actually consider . . . ?"

"You've not answered my question, Lord Farr." Meriel reminded him.

"It could be arranged very easily. I know Broxbridge Hall well. I visited there often as a lad. There is a certain passage which leads from the turret to a spot outside the castle walls. It was built at the same time the Hall was erected and meant to be used during times of siege. Later it became a hiding place for priests fleeing the wrath of Henry VIII and, subsequently, his daughter Elizabeth. During the Civil Wars, some of the Broxbridges loyal to Charles I, sheltered there. It is in reasonably good repair, though I think some of the masonry is crumbling. However, Rex cherishes bad memories of it." A smile flickered in his eyes. "Jemmy and I once dragged him in there as our prisoner and left him for half a day. He was terrified. He always was a timorous child. As I have explained, you'd need to make but one appearance and I'd be in the passage to get you out. Jemmy'll help me, I know. He's now a groom at the castle. We were great friends when we were small." He gave her a long, pleading look. "Will you do it, Miss Hathaway?"

Meeting his anxious eyes, Meriel was once more reminded of her encounter with Lord Hove. In truth, Lord Farr had saved her from a most horrid fate. Reaching her decision, she smiled valiantly up at him—realizing that she loved him—loved him enough to assume the disguise that would help him win the affections of the Incomparable. Repressing a sigh, she said, "Yes, Lord Farr, I shall be your Lady Blue."

# (3)

Battered by a strong sea breeze, the weathered sign that identified the small posting inn as the Three Gulls, swung back and forth, emitting a dismally squeaking moan. It was near five in the afternoon and the sky, which had been pale blue at times during the day and misty white at others, was filling with plump gray clouds scudding toward the horizon which was marked by high sand dunes and a restless wind-tossed strip of sea.

The ostlers and maid-servants who needed to be in the wide courtyard of the Three Gulls or, more simply The Gulls, as it was known in the neighboring village of Mablethorpe, put firm hands to hair, hats, or mobcaps. Such guests as were arriving climbed out of post-chaises, gigs, and wagons with nervous alacrity, and disappeared hastily through the commodious front door of the establishment. When a well-sprung, smart post-chaise appeared at the turn-off to The Gulls, there were some travelers who stopped to eye its shiny body and four handsome chestnuts in envious surprise. The rig looked far too expensive to be disgorging its occupants at so humble a hostel as The Gulls. Yet, once it had halted in the courtyard those who had stopped to stare were confused.

There was only one elderly groom to drive it, accompanied by a single, scrawny post-boy. There was neither an abigail nor a valet to accompany the couple, who emerged from the equipage. Still, both were dressed fashionably and seemed to be of the very first *ton* and, as several ladies were quick to agree, the sight of the woman was enough to stir the sensibilities of any observer. Garbed in deepest mourning and heavily veiled, she seemed the very· personification of Grief. It was not only her sable-hued bombazine garments that conveyed that impression, it was her evident lassitude.

More than merely leaning on her companion, she huddled against him. It was evident to those who saw them that without the strength of his sustaining arm, she might very well have collapsed at his feet. Her steps were slow and she pressed a dainty, black-edged handkerchief to her nose. Occasionally, her small, slender form was shaken by a torrent of weeping. As one elderly dowager remarked, it was a most affecting sight.

She and the lady with her, were also quick to admire the widow's escort, a tall, well-set-up young man, wearing a curly brimmed beaver hat and a dark, triple-caped traveling coat, which though long, afforded them a glimpse of tight buckskin breeches tucked into gleaming Hessian boots. His solicitude for the mourner was admirable. His face mirrored the deepest concern as he gently directed her faltering steps toward the inn door, patiently stopping and waiting while another paroxysm of grief shook her.

"Come, my dear," he was heard to say, as he brought her inside. "You must be brave."

A passing maid-servant, hearing the widow's reply, couched in the most heart-rending terms, confided it to the cook with tears in her own eyes. "H'it were that sad, Mrs. Goresby. 'Ow she said, 'H'I would H'I could lay with 'im in 'is cold, cold grave.'" Lifting her apron, the maid blew her nose loudly into its capacious folds.

"Um," Mrs. Goresby grunted. "You mark my words, May, she'll be dancin' a jig in another three months!"

"Oh, no," the girl protested. "'Ow can you say so, Mrs. Goresby?"

"You mark my words," the cook repeated, darkly. "Them as go in for all that h'outward show've their 'earts mended the soonest. It's h'always the way, An 'oo's this young man wi' 'er? Number Two, H'I'll be bound."

"Nothing of the sort," her informant flared. "'E's 'er brother. I 'eard 'im say so when 'e bespoke the upstairs parlor. 'E be takin' the poor little lady 'ome."

"Um . . ." Mrs. Goresby shot her a suspicious look. 'So they bespoke a private parlor, eh? H'I'd give a monkey to know 'ow they're carryin' on in h'it." •

"Mrs. Goresby!" May reddened. "You h'aint got no call to be so doubtin'. H'if you'd seen 'em ..."

"Now you listen to me, my girl," rasped the cook." You be sixteen an' h' I be three times that. When you're my h'age, ye'll not be takin' everythin' as 'ow it appears to be. Why're they at The Gull's? It h'aint for the likes of gentle-folk as 'ow you describe. It's a sight too far off the main road. 'Pears to me as 'ow they might 'ave somethin' to 'ide." Her eyes, narrow and squinting from too close proximity to the roaring open hearths of many kitchens, grew narrower still. "H'I'd give a monkey to know what they're a-doin' now."

Had Mrs. Goresby been able to see into the small upstairs parlor, she would undoubtedly have received her monkey's worth, for the "inconsolable widow" and her "brother," having seen the door close upon the ample form of the host, were seated at a small table, their hands over their mouths, as they strove to quell their laughter.

"Oh, oh, ohhhhh," Meriel moaned, when at last she could speak. "How well he left when he did. Another moment and I should have exploded and disgraced us, I know."

"Nothing of the kind," Lord Farr responded with a respectful look. "You carried it off admirably, as you always do. Though I must say that upon this occasion, rather than merely wearing the willow, you seemed to have donned a whole forest of 'em."

53

"B-But when I said that bit about wanting to . . . to be cold in his grave," Meriel gurgled, "my voice shook. Were you not alarmed?"

"Not at all," he assured her with an indulgent smile. "None but myself could have known it was with merriment. You are an excellent actress, ma'am."

"As you are an actor, my Lord," she replied.

"Shhhh," he cautioned, looking nervously around the small room. "I am not 'my Lord,' I am your brother Ulric Godwin."

"Then . . . I should not be ma'am." She reminded him.

"Of a truth, you are right, dear sister." He inclined his head. Casting another look around the parlor, he regarded its low ceiling and slanting floor, its worn carpet and battered furnishings with disfavor. "These accommodations leave much to be desired. I could wish you might be more comfortable after our hours on the road."

She smiled. "Come, I am very comfortable." Rising, she moved to the window. "It is much to my liking to have so admirable a view of the sea. If there were not so high a wind and the threat of rain, I should like to walk along the sands for a bit. I am sure it would not be out of my character."

"Indeed not," he agreed. "A solitary mourning figure upon the desolate shore." He rolled the sentence on his tongue and winked at her. "It could but inspire pity in the hearts of all beholders."

"That sounded very poetic." Meriel laughed. "Almost like Lord Byron."

"Perish the thought," he groaned.

"Do you not admire Lord Byron?"

"I've not had the pleasure of his acquaintance, but I have it on very good authority that he dines upon cold mashed potatoes and sleeps each night with his hair done up in curl-papers."

"Curl-papers!" Meriel looked at him aghast. "I cannot believe it."

"It's the truth for all that." Lord Farr grinned. "Fellow I know found him that way." Smiling into her shocked face, he added, "I'd not reflect upon it too much, my dear. Poets, you understand."

"But I don't. Except, of course, for Milton . . . whom I am quite sure did nothing to his hair."

"I shouldn't think so," he agreed. "A dim sort, Milton."

Meriel laughed. "Oh, I would my father might have heard you."

"Our father," he reminded her. "For the time, we share this cruel parent."

Reading sympathy in his frank gaze, she flushed. "Our father was not really cruel," she explained. "He suffered a great loss when my . . . er . . . our mother was killed."

"No need to inflict it upon you, whose loss was the greater, since it seems to have deprived you of both parents," he said, quietly.

Her flush deepened. Looking down quickly, she played with the large onyx mourning ring he had provided. "I . . . fear I have made out too great a case for myself," she said, ruefully.

"On the contrary. You've made none at

all. You are, in fact, a most unusual young woman. Our need for anonymity has resulted in a regrettable . . . er, bending of the proprieties. You should have a chaperon or, at the very least, an abigail, you know. Yet, you have made no demur, nor have you complained over indifferent hostelries far from the well-traveled roads. I can only offer you my felicitations. I can think of no other female of my acquaintance who would have born so many discomforts so bravely."

"Come," she replied quickly. "I have enjoyed every moment of our journey." She looked up at him, flushed and lovely from his praise, then hastily dropped her eyes, continuing self-consciously. "There is no reason why I should not have enjoyed it. The chaise is well-sprung and very comfortable and I've had an opportunity to see parts of the country that are new to me. Furthermore"—she glanced toward the window again"—we are close to the sea. I am very fond of the ocean, and I've not been near it since I was five."

He shook his head. "I think you are too easily pleased. I would we might have journeyed to Brighton, and you could have visited the Prince's Pavilion rather than this unprepossessing backwater."

"But it would not have suited your purposes half so well."

He stared at her for a long moment, finally saying slowly, "Miss Hathaway . . ."

"Meriel," she corrected swiftly.

"Meriel, of late I have begun to be afflicted with doubts as to the wisdom of my scheme. Indeed, if you'd prefer that I took you directly to my governess at Bath . . ."

"No," she interrupted sharply, then at his surprised look, she added, "I am game, my . . . brother. In fact, I am looking forward to seeing the castle and the passageway."

"Are you sure?" he asked earnestly. "Are you sure that you do not think this a preposterous and harebrained plan?"

"No, no," she assured him. "I am entirely convinced of its efficacy."

He looked relieved. "I will repeat that I find you a most unusual female," he said, gratefully then added, "The reason that I have ordered supper for seven is because I think you must rest."

"You are most considerate." She smiled.

"I hope that your chamber will be more comfortable than the one you occupied at the Crown and Garter."

Rising, she opened the door of the room alotted to her. "It looks to be so, and again, my windows face the sea," she started in and then, turning back, she said, "truly, my . . . brother, I assure you that I am quite enjoying myself." She gave him a mischievous smile. Before he could respond, she had whisked inside, closing her door behind her.

Standing against it, she put her hand to her heart, feeling its rapid pulsations in her throat as well as her in bosom. "If only . . ." She whispered to herself and paused, realizing there were many ways she could complete her statement. If only it were the beginning of the journey rather than the middle of it. If only they had four more days upon the road rather than two at the very most. If only they were going to the ends of the earth rather than York. If only there was no Miss Stansfield; but, in a sense, that was the most foolish of all her wishes. If there was no Miss Stansfield, there would have been no reason for their journey. Without the distant presence of the Incomparable, Meriel would be still in London, cowering in some cheap lodging house, blue-haired and forsaken. No, undoubtedly, Lord Farr would have taken her to Bath, tipped his hat to her, and passed out of her life forever. A fearsome prospect. Because of dear Miss Stansfield, she had spent two days in his company and could look forward to at least another week. Beyond that . . . She passed a hand over her eyes, almost as if she were blotting out a vision of the bleak future. She would not think about a time when she would not be able to turn her head and find him sitting beside her in the post-chaise or walking with her into an inn.

Truly, he had been inspired when he had decided she must be a "widow." Not only were her weeds a most effective disguise, it was lovely to be "bereaved" and in need of his sustaining arm. She flushed, hoping she had not overused that particular prop. Thinking about it, she was sure she had not. After all, he had unconditionally praised her performance and there had been a definite look of admiration in his eyes. She smiled, ruefully. If only it had been in recognition of her own charms. Her own charms! She shuddered, remembering at the same time, that she ought to remove her headdress and give her hair a chance to breathe.

With a little sigh of relief, she removed her veil and the swathing turban beneath it. Taking the pins from her hair, she let it fall about her shoulders. Then, with a gasp, she hastily locked the door.

"How could I have forgotten that incident at the Crown and Garter?" she chided herself, then giggled.

It was easy to giggle in retrospect, though, at the time, she had not been in the mood for it: The chambermaid, neglecting to knock, had come in with a basin of water just as Meriel was brushing her hair. Viewing those azure tresses, the maid had screamed and dropped the basin; she had been seized with spasms that rendered her temporarily incapable of speech or movement. Upon recovering her senses, the girl sped howling from the room, leaving both Meriel and Lord Farr in a quandary. Fortunately, as an apologetic if curious host was able to tell them, the girl was known to have imperfect understanding, and her amazing tale was not believed. It had been a very narrow escape.

Meriel felt sorry for the girl. It must have been quite shocking to see her hair which, thanks to Lord Farr's careful ministrations, was now thoroughly and evenly blue rather than the streaked product of Lord Algernon's eager but unpracticed hand.

She sighed, remembering her pleasure as Lord Farr had applied the dye. She had pretended that he was stroking her head. His touch had the gentleness she suspected a lover might possess, though, of course, she had never had that experience.

"And never will, either," she assured herself dolefully.

"Such a waste of time"—sneered her Other Self—"to fall in love with a man, who is hopelessly infatuated with the Incomparable.'

"Oh, if only I were an Incomparable," Meriel mourned.

"You are an Uncomparable. If you had had any sense, you'd have cut your hair off and . . ."

"Hush," Meriel hissed. "I am glad my hair is blue. Indeed, I am even glad of Algernon's attack. If it were not for that . . ."

"You'd not have embarked upon this mad course," averred Other Self hastily. "Mad it is, and you'll have only yourself to blame if and when . . ."

Meriel interrupted. "At least I shall have had this wonderful week."

Rigorously subduing the proddings of her conscience, she cast her mind back over the past two days with Lord Farr. She had been worried, she recalled, when, in the character of her comforting brother, he had elected to share a seat in the post-chaise rather than ride alongside the conveyance, as she knew he would prefer. Yet, he had not seemed bored with her company. On the contrary, they had covered many different subjects and, if he knew about her secluded life at Chalfont St. Giles, she had learned about his childhood, which was spent at a country estate near the town of Polesworth in Warwickshire. Oddly enough, they had found a certain common ground, for he, too, had been an only child with a single surviving parent—his mother, who was now deceased. Yet, she had the impression that Lord Lithwaite had often visited him, making up in part for the father he had lost while still in swaddling clothes. It was obvious that he was exceptionally fond of his uncle, but it was also obvious that he had been a lonely boy, for he had said, "When I marry, I shall see to it that I have several children. That is only fair, do you not agree, Meriel?"

She had·been thankful for her all-enveloping black veil, for she had felt her face grow warm as she nodded. "Yes, I do wholeheartedly agree." Indeed, she did. She wondered what he might have thought had he been able to share the indelicate vision that had flitted through her mind—a grassy sward populated with a trio of ruddy infants whose appearances combined his features with her coloring or, perhaps, the other way around.

Thinking about it now, she found herself fiercely resenting the uncle whose gambling had wasted her father's inheritance. "If I'd been an heiress, I should have been able to take my place in Society and . . ." She shook her head, dismissing the idea as unworthy of her. It did no good to pine over a long-distant past, just as it was equally useless to try and pierce the veils of the future, a future which did, however, contain one very vivid image of a frightened Miss Stansfield fleeing from the Specter of Broxbridge Hall directly into the waiting arms of Lord Farr.

"Driven there by me," Meriel whispered plaintively.

Jumping up and tossing her head, she muttered, "I shan't think about that. I shan't need to think about it for at least another two days." Moving to the window, she scanned the lowering sky, which had turned to ominous yellowish-gray. "Perhaps even longer," she mused. "It would be lovely if it were to storm . . ."

It did rain during the night, but Meriel, waking very early the following morning, looked out on a sea brightening under the rising sun. In her ears, was a chorus of squawks, shrieks, quacks, burbles, and tweets from a myriad of feathery throats. Slipping from her bed, she ran to the window and knelt to watch a great number of seabirds flying overhead and stalking about the beach. The tide had receded and doubtlessly there were crabs and other sea creatures caught in the wet sands, ripe for devouring. She smiled. Once more, she was reminded of her one other visit to the shore.

She and her parents had come to a small fishing village in Suffolk, a place of twisting cobblestoned streets and, in the harbor, moored boats, some with bright red sails. In the early morning, she and her mother had strolled along the water's edge. The small child had dared the waves to come and take her, dancing bravely after them as they rolled back toward the sea, running back as they came forward again.

Impulsively, Meriel sprang out of bed and dressed hastily, resenting the amount of time she had to spend bundling her hair into the turban and fixing the veil over the whole. Finally she was dressed. Closing her chamber door quietly behind her, she tiptoed across the parlor and down the stairs. Moments later, she emerged from the inn. Not only had the rain ceased, but the wind had been quelled to a pleasant breeze. She was a little surprised to find that the sea was farther than she'd thought seeing it from her window. Lured by the pounding of the waves and by the oddly beguiling sounds of the birds, she found a narrow path and followed it down to the dunes.

With a sigh of pleasure, Meriel hurried to the water's edge. It was obvious there had been a storm during the night, for great garlands of seaweed were washing onto the sand, and fragments of wood were strewn along the beach. More seaweed bobbed up and down in the bubbly waves, running up on shore in neat horizontals, intercepting and circumventing each other. Pulling back her veil, Meriel lifted her face to the salt-laden breeze. Suddenly, an importunate wave was at her toes and she was five years old again, leaping back from those watery tentacles, daring to taunt them. "You can't catch me!" she chanted under her breath, skipping to and fro. "You can't, can't, can't catch me!"

"Meriel!" The voice, unnaturally loud and peremptory, wrapped around her like the lash of a whip. Startled, she looked in its direction and found Lord Farr, hatless and clad only in his breeches and a shirt, which was gaping open to reveal his bare chest. He was hurrying toward her, his brows drawn together in a deep frown. "Come," he said, roughly, catching her by the arm. "Let us go back."

"My L . . . b-brother," she stuttered. "W-What can be amiss."

"Do not stop to question me now," he panted, then without further ado, he lifted her in his arms and hurried back up the path to the inn, not stopping in his headlong dash until they were inside The Gulls. Setting her down, he said curtly, "Come upstairs with me. There's something I'd have you see."

Wondering what was wrong, and a little frightened, she followed him up to the parlor.

"What . . . why . . . ," Meriel questioned.

Banging something down onto the table, he pointed to the window. "Look there."

Instead, Meriel, staring at the table saw a small pistol. Amazed, she said, "You . . . had a gun . . ."

"I have asked you to come to the window," Lord Farr reminded her curtly.

Obediently, she looked out. In the distance, she saw a group of tall, rough-looking men moving among the dunes, not far from where she had been standing. By their appearances, she guessed them to be fisherman or sailors. "Oh, dear," she said contritely. "I should not have lifted my veil. It was sadly out of character, but it was so early and . . ."

"Do you think that's why I fetched you?" he demanded incredulously. "I am only glad I awakened before they reached you. Must I tell you a second time, my dear Miss Hathaway, that you are not in Chalfont St. Giles."

She had a sudden vivid memory of Lord Hove's dissolute face. "You do not think they . . . would have harmed me?"

"I am grateful we did not need to find out.

My pistol would have been small protection among so many." He added heavily, "I must ask that in the future, you do not leave our rooms until I am ready to escort you."

Meriel hung her head. "I am sorry," she said in a small shamed voice. "I did not think . . ."

Placing his hand under her chin, Lord Farr tilted her face upward. "Come, come, I was not scolding you." He smiled. "Let me repeat the words my old nanny was wont to say to me so often I could repeat them in my sleep. 'It was for your own good.'"

"You are most kind, my L—brother," she whispered. "I do thank you."

He shook his head. "No need to . . ." he suddenly broke off, his hand straying to his open shirt. "Good God." He reddened. "It is my turn to ask your pardon, Miss . . . er Meriel. I'd forgotten I am but half-dressed. If you will excuse me . . ." Without waiting for her answer, he plunged into his chamber, closing the door behind him.

Meriel, looking after him, had an absurd desire to weep. Yet, at the same time, she was oddly happy. He had undoubtedly saved her again and at the expense of his strict sense of propriety. She could imagine how swiftly he must have thrown on his clothes and sped to her rescue. "He . . . was like a knight errant," she breathed dreamily.

"Come, come," jeered her Other Self. "Do not be likening yourself to any damsel in distress. How many young women with blue hair could he find in this kingdom?"

She emitted a short sharp sigh. It was a

quelling thought, but it was also eminently sensible. It brought to mind a vision of the lovely Miss Beatrix Stansfield. Blinking back a certain wetness in her eyes, Meriel hurried into her own chamber. A glance out of the window showed her that the sun was climbing higher. Soon it would be time to leave. "I am glad of it," she muttered defiantly. "I would this journey would be at an end!"

The horses' hooves sounded different, as did the wheels of the post-chaise. Meriel, who had been fitfully dozing in her corner, lifted her head and listened, realizing that they were rumbling over a wooden bridge. Looking out of the window, she saw an expanse of rippling water. "Where are we?" she inquired.

"We're crossing the Aire," Lord Farr informed her. "In a little less than an hour, we shall be in Selby." There was an edge of excitement to his voice that sent a pang through her, even though she had been steeling herself against this moment during the long hours of the previous day, and since they had left their inn outside of Torworth that morning. Still, she was able to say calmly, "Selby . . . then we are nearly to our destination."

"Yes," he agreed. "We'll rest in Selby tonight and cross the Ouse on the morrow. Broxbridge Village lies not far beyond York."

"We have made good time," she commented, inwardly glad that if her tone were not enthusiastic, at least it revealed nothing of her inner despair. In spite of her resolutions at the Three Gulls, she was not looking forward to the end of their journey. However, much to her chagrin, it was only too apparent that Lord Farr was more than eager to see it completed. She also feared he was finding her presence irksome and more of an encumbrance than an asset.

The delightful sense of camaraderie that had marked the earlier part of their journey was quite gone, and other than pointing out a famed church or ancient castle or some other landmark along the Great North Road, which he felt must be of particular interest to her, he had remained regrettably silent. Indeed, he had been so taciturn that Meriel feared he was angrier at her excursion to the shore than he had led her to believe. She had attempted to rectify matters by dutifully remaining in her chamber at the inn, where they had stayed last night, but still he had been sadly constrained at dinner. Counseling her to retire early, he had done the same, tapping on her door only moments past dawn. She sighed.

"Are you tired?" he demanded, more harshly than solicitously, she thought woefully.

"Not at all," she hastened to assure him.

"It has been a long journey. We've come nearly one hundred and seventy-six miles. I'd forgotten it was such a distance. I fear it has been very arduous."

"It has not been arduous," she assured him, quickly. "As I have told you, I have found it much to my liking. Though I am sorry if I have caused you undue worry."

"You've not caused me any worry, my

dear Miss Hathaway," he said. "I am deeply indebted to you and I can assure you that I will make it worth your while."

"You are very kind," she murmured, not trusting herself to speak louder lest her voice tremble and betray her. Turning away from him, she stared out at the passing scenery through a glaze of tears. He had not looked at her as he had spoken, and the coldness of his accents had chilled her to the bone. What could she have done, she wondered piteously.

She could hardly believe that the episode of the other morning had wrought so heavily upon him. Yet, to speak of payment in that cold, insulting way, quite as if she had been a servant in his employ . . . With difficulty, she bit down a little cry, realizing that that was exactly how he must regard her. He had, in effect, hired her as he might have hired an actress—to perform a role and, she reasoned ruefully, if she had been a real actress, certainly she would never have put him to the inconvenience of coming to her rescue. She would have known how to comport herself. Then, another disturbing thought rose in her mind. If he had not reached her before that band of men had sighted her, he might have been in jeopardy himself. In fact, he had said as much. Judging from his present attitude, he must have reached the conclusion that she was more of a handful than he had anticipated. It might also have occurred to him that he had been too friendly to her. His was a gregarious and expansive nature. It was difficult for him to maintain the proper distance between himself and anyone sharing his carriage, but, obviously, he had decided he must surmount this difficulty and put her in her place or, at least, keep his own.

Though she thought her analysis of his motives quite brilliant, she also found it extremely lowering to her spirits. In fact, she was so cast down that she wished she had the courage to flee from his presence.

"Hold on." It was her Other Self commanding her, and in a much different vein than usual. Rather than being derisive, it had turned practical. "You could not be such a coward or so negligent of your responsibilities," it chided. "You have agreed to help him. As he has reminded you, he will pay you well. You are presently . . ." she glanced out of the window, "some one hundred and seventy-seven or so miles from London. You have blue hair. You not only owe it to him to keep your part of the bargain, it is a financial necessity. My advice to you is to act out his 'Lady Blue,' and do it to the best of your ability. Let him know that his judgment was not in error when he chose you. Remember, even Papa praised your reading of Milton and Shakespeare. He said you spoke the lines with intelligence and conveyed the meaning with dramatic effect. As Lady Blue, you'll not have to speak. Indeed, there will be nothing to it."

"Are you cold?" Lord Farr inquired.

"N-no," she stuttered.

"You shivered," he stated, almost in an accusing voice.

"It . . . was a goose walking over my grave," she explained diffidently.

"Nonsense," he said, crossly.

"Undoubtedly," she replied. Certainly, she had no intention of explaining to him that in that particular moment, she had been visited by a peculiar sense of impending doom. He would have told her it was only her imagination, which was something she much preferred to believe.

# (4)

The cumbersome machinery of the tall "Up-and-Down" clanked loudly as its load of passengers giggled and screamed within its swinging wooden seats. Three of its "arms" went upward as the other three went down, allowing one pale-faced couple to disembark. At the top of the mechanism, another pair of joy-riders swung perilously over the small fairgrounds, rewarded by a view of the town of Selby, the silvery expanse of the River Ouse and the ruins of an ancient abbey. However, Meriel, standing near Lord Farr, had the idea the riders' frenzied shrieks indicated that they were deriving more pain than pleasure from their vantage point. It was really very noisy, she thought. In addition to the plaints of those who had braved the "Up-and-Down," there were the howls of others who were currently enjoying the dubious thrills of its sister machine, the "Round-About."

Mingling with these were the salutations of hawkers selling dolls and other goods; the deeper, more sonorous voice of the Pieman, making his way through the multitudes with a load of freshly baked wares; the hoarse roars of the beasts penned in the steel cages of the "menagerie" attached to the Hodgkins Circus; and the falsetto tones of those who worked the "Punch and Judy Show," which was, evidently, at the point where the redoubtable Punch was warring with the Devil and Death. Indeed, everywhere one looked, someone was raising his voice to summon the crowds. Games of "Roly-Poly" and dice were offered. Oddities, such as an India-Rubber Man and a Monkey Woman were luridly depicted on posters hung outside tents. A gypsy leading a huge black bear, which was lumbering along on its hind feet, invited all and sundry to watch Toto dance; and, nearby, a group of small, ragged urchins screamed with fearful delight while a "Fire-Eater" applied a burning torch to his mouth. Above the babble, Meriel could hear the valiant efforts of a small brass band as it struck up a march.

If she were bewildered by the noise and the confusion, Meriel was no less bemused by her companion's miraculous change of attitude. It had come about minutes after arriving in the courtyard of the Gilded Cock to discover that a large plot of ground behind the establishment had been given over to the Hodgkins Circus and Carnival. On seeing it,

Lord Farr's bad temper had vanished as inexplicably as it had appeared, and smiling gaily down at Meriel, he had exclaimed, "By **God**, I've not seen one of these since I was a lad!" Almost anxiously, he'd asked, "Should you like to go and view it?"

"Oh, I would very much," she had agreed, eagerly. Then, belatedly assailed by caution, she ventured to remark," But we are—very near to York, are we not?"

He had laughed. "No matter, I cannot imagine any of my acquaintances—least of all my highly proper Cousin Rex and Miss Stansfield ever coming here."

Though Meriel's knowledge of his Yorkshire acquaintances stopped with Miss Stansfield, she could agree that the entertainment in question would not attract the local Quality. "I should not think they would much enjoy it." she commented.

"And you?" There was a note of anxiety in his voice again. "Are you sure you will?"

"Oh, yes," she'd said. "I've never been on a fairgrounds."

He had been surprised. "But surely, they must have come to Chalfont St. Giles."

"Oh, they did," she agreed, "but Papa . . ."

He had nodded quickly, giving her arm a little squeeze. "I understand. Then it's time you had the opportunity to visit one. Only, I adjure you, hold tightly to your reticule. These places are the natural haunts of pickpockets and other undesirables. At Bartholomew Fair, the thieves have grown very bold and have been known to rip the clothing from unwary females. However, I doubt we'll meet such criminals here.

Still, you must keep hold of my arm and not go wandering off by yourself, my sister."

"Oh, I shall not," she assured him.

She was clinging to that proffered arm at present, and if she were to be truthful, she was finding that more exciting than anything that was taking place around her. Though it was close to the twilight hour, Meriel felt as though the sun were still brightly shining.

Lord Farr, who had been glancing around, suddenly yelled, "Come, I think I see a Conjurer's tent over there," he pointed. "Should you like to witness some legerdemain?"

"Oh, indeed, I should like nothing better," she said, and was rewarded by his grateful smile.

"Come then," he said, and skirting the crowds as best he could, he led her toward a tent fronted by a poster on which was emblazoned, "THE GREAT KHAN AND HIS DEATH-DE-FYING BULLET-CATCHING ACT."

"Ah," he exclaimed, "now there is something I certainly did not expect to find in a traveling circus!"

Meriel read the words with some trepidation, "B-Bullet . . . catching," she quavered. "How would he do that?"

"In his teeth." Lord Farr pointed to the poster. "See, they are showing him in the very act."

Looking at the picture more closely, she saw a turbaned gentleman with a bullet clamped between his large white teeth. He was depicted smiling broadly. "I . . . don't see . . ." she began, only to be startled by the sound of a shot. "Oh!" she exclaimed, tightening her clasp on Lord Farr's arm. There was a moment of silence, then a wild burst of applause, accompanied by cheers from inside the tent.

"He's done it!" Lord Farr exclaimed. "It's a notable illusion. I've seen it attempted only once before—in London last winter. It was done by a pair of Indian jugglers. Maybe this Khan is one of them, or, perhaps, . . . but I'll not speculate. Let us see."

Some fifteen minutes later, they were inside the tent, seated on a bench just below the raised platform where the Conjuror worked. The little stage was wonderfully lighted. A bluish glow played over the magician's face, and if he were neither so tall nor so handsome as he had been depicted on the poster, still he was impressive in his snow-white turban and his colorful satin robes. He was assisted by a young woman in a cerise sari, which sparkled with golden threads. Numerous gold and silver bangles, some heavy with coins, were on her wrists, and there were bells on her ankles that tinkled as she walked back and forth at the behest of the Great Khan.

The magician had not yet come to the bullet-catching illusion. He'd produced a rabbit from a hat and was now involved in bringing out an endless amount of bright silken scarves from a seemingly empty box. "That," Lord Farr explained in a whisper, "is the 'Silk Trick.'"

"It's amazing," Meriel whispered back. "How does he do it?"

Lord Farr smiled at her indulgently. "It's

not difficult. You need only have dexterous fingers . . . so." Reaching into his pocket, he produced a shilling and before her eyes made it disappear and reappear in his other hand.

"Oh," she breathed and then gasped, for he had taken the same coin from her veil. Before she could comment, he nudged her.

"I think," he said in a voice that managed to be both relieved and excited, "that he is through with the preliminaries."

Looking up, she saw that the Conjurer's assistant had gone off-stage. The girl returned in a matter of seconds, carrying a case of dueling pistols, which she placed on the small table that had supported the other paraphernalia of magic.

Suddenly, the light changed, glowing red instead of blue, and from somewhere off-stage, there was a drum roll which ended as another man, garbed in green satin evening clothes, which were heavily trimmed with gold lace, leaped up onto the stage. He turned, a narrow, saturnine contenance toward the audience.

"Ladeez and Gentlemen," he announced, loudly. "You are about to witness one of the most spectacular feats of all time. Through the power of his Black Art, handed down to him from his father and his father before him—unto seven generations—the great magician, the Conjuror of Conjurors, the marvelous magical, miraculous sage from the fabled land of Samarkand: The Great Khan, will now perform his dangerous, death-defying act of catching a real bullet, shot at him from one of these dueling pistols. How will he catch it? Not in his hand, but in his teeth, Ladeez 'n' Gentlemen.

76

In his Teeth! Now, I shall choose a member of this audience who will examine these guns and ascertain for himself and for the rest of you whether or not they are loaded with real bullets. Bullets, which, being discharged from their muzzles, can enter a man's heart and kill him instantaneously. It will be a bullet from one of these pistols. Chosen, I say, by a member of the audience—a man, who has never seen the Great Khan, a man, who walked into this tent this evening. This man will now wield the power of life and death over the Great Khan! Now, at the command of the Great Khan, I shall choose this man, who might be his executioner." Stepping forward, the Barker scanned the faces of the audience, and, as he did, there was a stir among them and a number of eager offers, accompanied by wildly waving hands. However, the Barker made no move to accept any of these bids. Instead, he continued to scan the crowd. Then, finally, he pointed directly at Lord Farr. "I think . . . yes, I am rather sure that it must be you, sir. Would you be good enough to examine these pistols and tell us if everything is in order?"

Lord Farr rose at once. "I should be delighted," he answered courteously.

The assistant moved to the table and picking up the case of pistols handed it to the Barker, who forthwith passed them to Lord Farr.

Lord Farr looked at them closely, and then, with a little note of surprise in his tone, he said, "They are quite in order. Certainly, I should not like to have either of them pointed at my mouth."

"Did you hear that, Ladeez 'n' gentlemen!" called the Barker.

He received another chorus of affirmatives; some loud and some soft.

"Are you willing to accept the judgment of this fine young man?" he demanded.

The audience responded with another round of affirmatives, though one man topped the rest with an impatient, "Come on, get on with h'it."

"Ah, hah." The Barker grinned. "There's one among us who is thirsting for blood. A proper descendant of the Romans who once occupied these parts. Very well, the Great Khan will endeavor to lay down his life for you, sir." Stepping back, he replaced the case of pistols on the table and signaled for the girl to come forward.

Gliding to the table, she removed one of the pistols from the case and stood holding it. The drums began to roll again, and she stepped to the far side of the stage, waiting while the Great Khan took his place directly across from her. She was about to take aim when the Barker suddenly made a motion and the drumbeats ceased.

Stepping to the front of the stage again, he addressed the audience. "Ladeez'n' gentlemen, it has occurred to me that you might not believe that these pistols are properly primed and loaded. Too, you may have doubts about the young lady's aim. It is the wish of the Great Khan that you see a little exhibition of her skill as a markswoman. She will now shoot the pip from this playing card that I hold in my hand."

There were more stirrings amongst the crowd as, with elaborate *sang-froid*, the Barker took his place beside the Magician, holding up a card marked with the Ace of Spades, which he displayed to the audience. "If the young lady misses, I have directed that my body be sent home to my native village," he said solemnly, as he held up the card toward the girl.

"Oh!" Meriel edged closer to Lord Farr. "I wish . . . he . . . he wouldn't . . ."

Neville Farr put a friendly arm around her. "Do not be frightened," he whispered, as the drums began to roll again.

Slowly the assistant lifted her hand, took aim, and fired. The Barker stepped forward holding up the bullet-holed card, to the relief and loud delight of the onlookers.

"You see," Lord Farr murmured, as the applause died down. "It is nothing but an illusion."

"An illusion," Meriel repeated musingly. "An illusion," she added in her mind. She needed to tell herself that, because his arm was so tight about her shoulders. Consequently, it was easy, far too easy to believe that he cared for her, Meriel Hathaway, rather than the beautiful Beatrix, who was not more than a few miles distant, enjoying the ducal splendors of Broxbridge Hall. Thinking about Miss Stansfield, Meriel was sure that beauty would never deign to accompany Lord Farr to a circus, much less step inside a magician's tent. On the other hand, she would never cause him any undue anxiety.

If Beatrix consented to accept his suit, he

could be sure that she would always conduct herself with the greatest propriety. Certainly, he would never be called upon to rescue her from a dissolute Lord Hove or chase her across the sands to ... Meriel's melancholy reflections ceased, as Lord Farr nudged her again.

"Look at the stage."

Raising her eyes, she realized that the drums were rolling again. The Great Khan was in his corner and the girl was lifting her pistol. The audiences ceased to mutter and fidget; everyone was preternaturally silent. The girl took aim, waited a split second while the Great Khan was seen to brace himself, his mouth half-open, his teeth gleaming. But, Meriel noted that the grin she'd seen on the poster was absent. The Great Khan looked sober, even a little fearful. Then, there was a loud noise, the gun jerked in the assistant's hand, there was the acrid smell of gunpowder in the air, and a great groan swept through the tent. For the Khan had staggered back, raising a trembling hand to his mouth. For a second there was total silence, then wild applause and cheers; for the magician straightened himself, stepped to the front of the stage, and opened his mouth wide. A cartridge was caught between his strong white teeth. Extricating it, he held it up so that everyone in the tent might see.

The Barker moved forward. "Ladeez 'n' gen-gentlemen, I hope you have enjoyed this spectacle of spectacles. Now, it is my duty to inform you that the performance is at an end!"

Lord Farr, helping Meriel to her feet, smiled gaily. "Did I not tell you it was an illusion?" he demanded.

"I wonder how it was done," she breathed. "It seems highly perilous."

"It only seems that way," he answered lightly. "Just as you, my dear Meriel, will only seem to be a ghost."

She tensed. Again she had forgotten her reason for being with him, and for a second, she was wildly resentful because he had brought it back to her mind. She tried to banish this sentiment as being unworthy of her. He could not help loving Miss Stansfield any more than she could help loving him. It behooved her to be understanding. She smiled. "I can only hope I shall be as successful as the Great Khan."

"I am sure ..." he began and paused, for the Barker had come down from the stage and stood in front of them. "You wished to speak to me?" Lord Farr asked.

"If you please, sir," the man said deferentially. "The Great Khan would be most gratified if he might thank you personally for your participation in his performance. If you would deign to come up on to the stage?"

Lord Farr inclined his head. "Rather I should be overjoyed to offer him my congratulations on his superb showmanship," he said, eagerly.

The Barker raised his hand in a graceful gesture. "If you and your lady would come this way, sir."

They followed him up a pair of stairs onto

what proved an insubstantial platform, which shook perilously under their every step as they made their way to where the Conjuror stood talking with his assistant. As they drew nearer, Meriel saw that the illusion the Great Khan projected was not confined to his tricks alone. The stage, which had appeared to be a dark and mysterious cavern, was far more shallow than it seemed from below. She also noted that many of the accouterments that the magician used looked cheap and tawdry under closer scrutiny. The Great Khan, himself, was both more slight of build and older than she had expected. The light had served to obliterate the deep lines in his forehead; it had been equally kind to the girl, who, until that moment had seemed no older than Meriel. Now it was evident that she was far closer to thirty than to twenty. Her mouth drooped wearily and there was a harried look in her eye. However, she smiled at Lord Farr's appreciative remarks.

Another surprise awaited Meriel when the Khan spoke. She had expected an Indian accent, but instead she heard the rich, fruity tones often associated with a Shakespearean actor as, in answer to Lord Farr's compliments, he said, "I value your opinion, young sir, for it seems to me that you must be one of the Brotherhood."

"The Brotherhood?" Lord Farr raised his eyebrows.

"Of magicians," the Khan added.

Lord Farr stiffened, looking at him with a mixture of embarrassment and surprise. "You could not have seen . . ." he began.

"But I did," the magician answered with a

hint of laughter threading his tones. Pressing his hands together, he bowed and brought them toward his brow, intoning, "The Great Khan is all-seeing, all-knowing. He has the mystic Third Eye in the middle of his forehead." Dropping his hands, he laughed. "Yes, I saw you manipulating the coin. I was most impressed." Indicating a pack of cards on the table, he asked, "Are you as proficient with cards as you are with coins?"

Lord Farr reached for the cards and executed a complicated shuffle that caused Meriel to gasp in surprise. "I know a few tricks," he said, casually.

The magician and his assistant exchanged a glance. "More than a few, I should say. I would not be surprised if you could duplicate many of the effects, I displayed tonight."

"I've yet to catch a bullet in my teeth." Lord Farr grinned.

"But that can be easily learned," the Khan said, seriously. "It is not dangerous, I assure you. However, be that as it may, I had a reason for asking you to come up here, sir."

"A reason?" Lord Farr questioned.

The Great Khan nodded and looked at him regretfully. "Yes, though now we meet face to face, I feel that I know what your answer will be, even before I voice my question. However, I will continue on the slim chance that . . ."

"Do get to the point, 'enry," begged the girl.

The Great Khan shot her an annoyed look. "Ah, yes, my dear, very well. You see, sir, last week, my First Assistant became ill. A promising lad he was, too, very promising. He also had dexterous fingers and was able to fill in for me on occasion. No matter, he became ill and we were forced to leave him behind in Whitely. We have missed him sorely—for a great deal of his work has fallen upon the slender shoulders of my young wife. If . . . you were in the need of er . . . gainful employment . . ."

Lord Farr shook his head. "Your offer is highly flattering, sir, but I am not."

"I told you 'e wouldn't be h'interested," the girl sighed. "Anyone can see 'e's a toff."

The Khan gave her a quelling look. "Yes, I quite realize that, my dear," he admitted. "But, occasionally, even the Quality are down on their luck. You have a fine pair of hands young man. Might I enquire where you learned to conjure?"

"There was a retired magician who lived near my home when I was a lad," Lord Farr explained. "He was pleased to give me some little instruction."

"And you chose to do nothing with it?" The Khan shook his head. "It is a pity, sir. With your combination of appearance and address, as well as your manual dexterity, I would think you might reap rich rewards."

Lord Farr bowed. "Such praise coming from a performer of your abilities, sir, have provided me with all the reward, I deserve." Taking Meriel's arm, he continued, "But now, I think my sister and I must let you rest."

Accompanied by a flurry of exuberant farewells, they made their way out of the tent. Lord Farr was in high spirits. "Well . . . if I should lose my blunt, I'll not need to become a public charge." He laughed.

"No, indeed," Meriel agreed. "I am sure you would prosper. You could call yourself the 'Mighty Mogul.'"

"The very thing," he exclaimed. "You could be my Lady Assistant in veils and bangles."

"I should like that above all things," Meriel giggled. "However, I must warn you that I am not a very good shot."

"Nor. I'll warrant, is she," he replied.

Meriel looked up at him, wide-eyed. "Was that also a trick? I mean—shooting the pip from the card?"

"Can you think, my lovely innocent, that it was not?" He raised his eyebrows. "Can you imagine that the Barker would have held it so coolly in his two fingers, had the threat been real? It is all illusion." Putting his hand on his chest, he struck a mock heroic attitude and, in the fulsome tones of the Khan, he declaimed, "All life is but an illusion, my dear Meriel." Dropping his pose, he looked around him. "It is growing late. We'd best get back to the inn, if we're to sup and rise early. We've a long day ahead of us tomorrow."

She stifled a tiny sigh, thinking that she was growing wonderfully adept at concealing the surges of disappointment that were engendered by his casual references to their ultimate goal. "Yes, I think we must," she agreed, and even managed to imbue her next comment with a certain eagerness. "I am in hopes of seeing Broxbridge Hall—from afar, I mean."

"Oh, yes, you'll be able to see it," he said, without enthusiasm. "It stands on a hill, well above any surrounding foliage. I think, however, that you will hardly be titillated by the sight, since it is a singularly ugly pile of rock, which only my cousin seems to admire."

He had spoken with an uncharacteristic waspishness, which depressed her even more, since it hinted of the frustration he must be feeling in regards to Miss Stansfield's sojourn within that pile.

Lord Farr quickened his step, to the point where Meriel had to hurry to keep up with him. She was managing this lively pace until her eyes caught sight of a banner reading "MADAME ASTRA, SEES ALL!" Beneath the lettering was a large representation of a palm, heavily inscribed with black lines, each adorned with an astrological symbol. Depicted directly beneath the palm was a spread of playing cards, the Ace of Hearts, King of Diamonds, Queen of Spades, and Jack of Clubs. Beside them was the crude drawing of a teacup.

"Oh," she said, coming to an abrupt stop and looking at the tent longingly. Their maid at home had been much in the habit of visiting an old woman, who ostensibly sold herbs, but whose main souce of income came from her ability to read the cards. Supposedly, the girl had received some extremely accurate information about her intended husband and even the date on which they were to be wed. Though Meriel's father had sneered at these revelations, Meriel had longed to visit the lady. Now, she discovered within herself a most pressing desire to know more about her future.

A hand fell on her shoulder and an impatient voice rasped, "Did I not tell you we must stay together? Why did you . . . ?" Lord Farr suddenly broke off mid-sentence as he, too, saw the sign. Throwing back his head, he laughed and in a much gentler tone, inquired, "Should you like to have your fortune told?"

Meriel hastened to answer, "No, please, I am sorry that I fell behind. I know you are in a hurry and . . ."

"Not so much in a hurry as all that," he assured her. "Go, consult your sibyl." Reaching into his pocket, he brought out several coins, pressing them into her hand. "Naturally, you will need to cross her palm with silver."

"But . . ." Meriel stood aside as a young couple, arms around each other's waists, came giggling from the tent.

"Go," Lord Farr gave her a little push. "Your pythoness is free. I shall wait out here. I'll be much interested to hear what she'll tell you about your 'deceased' husband." He gave Meriel's veil a mischievous tweak.

"Oh!" Meriel shot him a guilty look. During the time they had been together in the fairgrounds, she had been so happy that she had forgotten the role she was supposed to be enacting. "I am afraid I have shed my willows."

"No matter. Surely, a widow has a right to seek some amusement during her period of mourning. I have sighted others of the bereaved among the merrymakers today."

She smiled gratefully. "You are most forbearing with me, sir, but I have been remiss. Tomorrow, I shall do better." With a shy smile, she stepped into the tent.

The interior proved very dark, so dark that

it was a moment before her eyes could adjust to the gloom. Then, some distance away, she saw a small round table covered with a brightly colored cloth on which were inscribed strange cabalistic signs. It was edged with gold fringe and on it was a small glass containing a lighted candle. Sitting at it was a woman in the vivid garments of a gypsy. A yellow scarf was tied around her head, while huge golden hoops dangled from her ears. Seemingly unaware of Meriel, she peered into a small, very clear crystal ball mounted on an ebony stand. There was something so rapt in her attitude that Meriel hesitated to disturb her. Casting a nervous glance behind her, she was about to leave the tent when the woman, suddenly, looked up, shooting her head forward in a movement curiously reminiscent of a striking serpent.

"You have come to see into the future, Little One?" she asked in a deep, melodious voice.

"Y-Yes," Meriel faltered, finding the lady more intimidating than she had imagined she might be.

"Then, you must come closer, and you must approach without fear." The Gypsy beckoned to her, imperiously. "Come," she ordered.

Discovering that her curiosity was greater than her fear, Meriel moved forward to stand across the table from the gypsy. Seeing a little stool pushed halfway under the table, she asked, "Do I sit down?"

"Please."

Then, as Meriel took her place, the Gypsy raised dark, hooded eyes and scanned her face closely. "Ahhhhh, I see that you are the One." she nodded.

"The . . . one?" Meriel questioned.

The gypsy leaned forward, and lifting the glass with its tiny flickering flame, she stared into Meriel's eyes. "You are the one for whom I have waited this day. Each morning I am told there will be one, who is not like the others who consult me. She is neither a giggling girl seeking to learn the identity of her future husband, who is the boy she has known all of her life and whom she could not escape if she chose, nor is she a silly woman, grown idle and bored and cheating her good man with her dreams of the lover she will never find.

"The one for whom I have waited this day is in trouble. She walks with sorrow and grief, but it is not the false grief that she exhibits in her garments, which are as sheep's clothing on the wolf. Though, instead, I must say that the sheep is in wolf's clothing, for she is no wolf but a lamb, and her grief is true and deep. It is the grief of the unloved and the lonely, lonelier now that love walks beside her but does not know his arrows pierce her heart. But love, my Little One, is like a plant. The seeds must be nurtured and are being nurtured, though as yet no tender green sprig has pierced the soil and gained the sunlight. Yet, there is a time for nurturing and a time for growing, and a time for blossoming. And the little grieving one, will know all these times." The Gypsy paused, and again she scanned Meriel's face. "But before that there is danger and deceit— and there is danger in the deceit and deceit in the danger. I see bloodshed and pain, pain and bloodshed. I see tears and a parting. I see losing and winning. I see good and I see evil —and I see a short journey and a longer one. I see a weary wait and a cold fire, but its flames will warm you. Now, I am told that I must tell you no more. No, I am to remind you that there is the time of blossoming." The Gypsy ceased speaking and, then, for the third time she peered into Meriel's face. "I hope you have listened. Yet, I think you will not remember much of what I have said, but when the time comes for remembering, perhaps, you will remember what Madame Astra has seen." She smiled. "That is all, little lady. Cross my palm with silver and I will bid you good evening—and, since there is no stopping that which must go forward, I wish you God speed on your journey of the morrow."

Her words had been strange and almost spell-binding. Meriel had listened carefully, but now, as she pressed all the coins Lord Farr had given her into the Gypsy's hand, she was already trying to remember what had been said and already forgetting. She rose. "I-I bid you a good evening, too, M-Madame Astra," she blurted. Then, for reasons she could not name, she sped from the tent. Running blindly from the entrance she was caught and held by Lord Farr.

"What's amiss?" he demanded with a concerned frown.

She clung to him for a moment. "She . . . I do not know . . ." With an effort, she tried to laugh. "It was nothing."

He continued to frown. "It seems she's

frightened you," he said, sharply. Releasing Meriel, he took a step toward the tent.

"No!" Meriel clutched his arm. "She did not frighten me. She . . ."

"What did she tell you?"

"I am not sure. She . . . knew there would be a journey tomorrow."

"A journey?" his frown vanished and a little knowing smile took its place. "Did she also mention a tall, dark man?" he asked sarcastically.

"No," Meriel said.

"Ah, well." He laughed. "I expect she varies the pattern a bit. But you're not to take any of it seriously, my dear. I assure you, it's all moonshine."

"Moonshine . . ." Meriel repeated and found laughter easier to achieve. "I think you must be right, for I vow, I can hardly remember anything she said."

"It's just as well. Come along."

As she took his arm, Meriel did remember one phrase from the gypsy's patter. Something about love walking beside her, not knowing that his arrows pierced her heart. That, she thought sadly, was not moonshine.

# (5)

On a grassy hillock a few miles beyond
the village of Broxbridge, Meriel and Lord
Farr, respectively mounted on a mettlesome
little chestnut mare and a large gray gelding,
stared at Broxbridge Hall. It was, she thought,
an awesome sight. Stark and massive against a
horizon embellished by gold-edged clouds, its
battlements dyed blood-red by the rays of the
declining sun; it was very easy to imagine the
fear that the mighty stronghold must have generated in olden times. The lords who had
dwelt in that stony vastness had been in a
position to wield the power of life and
death over those who dwelt in the castle's
shadow.

"There is the North Turret." Lord Farr indicated, raising his hand.

She looked at its crenelated summit. "It is very high."

"You are not afraid of heights, I hope?" he asked, anxiously.

"Oh, no." She could assure him easily. "I love being up in high places. There used to be a tree in our garden that I was wont to climb. No, I was thinking of that poor girl who was pushed to her death. It is such a very long way to fall."

"Yes, if the tale be true."

"Do you think it was not?"

He shrugged and smiled. "Even as an acorn becomes an oak, so do other small kernels sprout great trunks and many leafy branches through the centuries. But . . . for our purposes, it's best we believe in our azure specter."

"I, myself, find it far easier to believe in the murder than that those thick walls are seamed with secret passages."

"The 'sally forths' proved very useful when the castle was under siege."

"The 'sally forths,' did you say?" she questioned. "What are they?"

"It's a type of secret passage. As I think I mentioned, it was built at the same time that the castle was erected. A soldier could leave the North Turret, slip into the passage, make his way to that point behind the walls and 'sally forth' to find food with which to relieve a starving garrison."

"How horrid to starve people into submission!" Meriel exclaimed. "The Dukes of Broxbridge must have had some very cruel neighbors."

"They, too, were cruel," Lord Farr told her. "They used to come pounding out of the castle to prey on wealthy travelers, and they made regular raids on the surrounding villages, carrying off their prettiest women across their saddle-bows."

Meriel chuckled. Meeting his surprised look, she explained, "It's well for Miss Stansfield that times and dukes have changed. I cannot imagine that she would have enjoyed so precipitate a wooing."

He laughed appreciatively. "Nor would my Cousin Rex. He's a damned dull dog and a stickler for the proprieties. In fact, I cannot understand why—" he broke off abruptly and wheeling his horse around, he said shortly, "Have you looked your fill?"

She guessed he must be thinking of Miss Stansfield and primed by her own yearning for him, she could imagine what a terrible disappointment it had been when the Incomparable had accepted the Duke's invitation. Now that they were near the Hall, she knew his suffering must have doubled, for the woman he loved was shut away from him, behind those ramparts. It occurred to her that in asking to see the castle, she had poured salt into his wounds. She said contritely, "Oh, yes, I've seen quite enough. You were so kind to show it to me."

His dark eyebrows drew together in a frown and his next words seemed to confirm her suspicions. "My dear Meriel, you must not always be talking of my 'kindnesses.' It is I who am in your debt." He stared at the castle

94

and then, abruptly, administered a slap to his horse's flanks "Let us return to the inn."

They rode in companionable silence back to Broxbridge Village. They had put up at the Thistle and Shrub, a small but comfortable hostelry, which had the advantage both of being off the main road and of being patronized mainly by wealthy farmers and professional people, such as lawyers and doctors. More affluent travelers and the stage coaches stopped at the larger Broxbridge Arms.

Upon their return, they found supper awaiting them in the small suite of rooms they occupied on the second floor. It consisted of a pasty, a well-cooked herbed chicken, fresh young peas and potatoes, rounded out with a pudding and fresh strawberries. It was better than many of the meals they had had in other inns along the road, but Lord Farr took no more than a bite from each dish and drank but a single glass of wine. It seemed only minutes before he rose from the table, saying abruptly, "I'm off to find Jemmy."

"Jemmy?"

"At the Hall . . . Jemmy Soutar," he said, almost impatiently.

"Oh, yes, of course." She smiled. "Your friend. Shall you be gone long?"

"Not long. Though I shall have to take a circuitous route. I dare not be seen." There was an undercurrent of excitement in his speech and his eyes sparkled. He smiled at her, but she had the impression that rather than seeing her, a vision of Miss Stansfield was shimmering before him. However, he said,

95

"I bid you a good evening, Meriel." Then astonishingly, he kissed her hand. "Let me say again, my dear, how very grateful I am to you. I'll not forget how much I owe to you."

"But, I have done nothing yet, my Lord."

"On the contrary, you have done much; not only by your complicity—but by your encouragement." As he opened the parlor door, he added, "You are, as I have so often said, a most unusual young woman."

Immediately after the door closed on him, Meriel went to her own chamber and, drawing up a chair, sat at the window staring out at the darkening sky. The nearly full moon was rising. Its radiant beams illuminated the broken walls of an ancient cloister some distance away, and, shining through the frame of a rose window, its light threw patterned shadows across the thick spring grass. Though, usually, she would have been enthralled by the sight, Meriel scarcely noticed it. In her mind's eye, she was following him as he rode toward the hall. She wondered if he would try and obtain a glance of Miss Stansfield. Since he knew the castle so well, she imagined there must be many places where he could see and yet be unseen by those in residence. If he did take such a chance, she prayed he would be spared a sight of the Incomparable flirting and laughing with his cousin.

She shook her head, wondering how Miss Stansfield could have kept him dangling so long. Yet, perhaps, she did not realize what she would be losing if she spurned his suit. She had never had the opportunity of spending long days with him. She did not know what a delightful companion he could be.

Meriel rose abruptly and moved about her room, wishing she might walk to the cloister, but that was out of the question. She had given her word to Lord Farr. In that moment, she wished that she had not, for she felt very restless and, she suddenly realized, strangely depressed.

Of course that was easily explainable. She was nervous at the thought of her upcoming impersonation and, too, her time with Lord Farr was drawing to a close. No, it was more than that. This sensation was not new to her. She had termed it "a goose walking over her grave," and Lord Farr had been annoyed. He would have been even more annoyed had he been able to see into her mind at present, for the more she thought about it, the more her feeling of "wrongness" increased. Yet, possibly, there was a logical explanation for that, too: Madame Astra. The Gypsy had predicted that she would remember little of what she had told her, and it was true that she could recall only fragments of her prediction. But she recalled the mention of "pain and bloodshed." Meriel bit back a little frightened cry. Supposing the pain were not her own . . . supposing dear Lord Farr was in danger?

"No," she whispered. "Please no," and was reminded of something her old nurse had once told her about "borrowing trouble." With effort she forced herself to look at her situation calmly and logically. There was really only one thing that could go wrong. They might discover that she was not a ghost. That would certainly be embarrassing, but, as everyone knew Lord Farr's bent for practical joking, no one would be more than surprised. She could imagine that once she was apprised of the reasons behind the prank, Miss Stansfield might even find it highly flattering. That was a melancholy conclusion, but it did not carry with it any particular sense of fear.

"I am being very foolish," Meriel said, firmly.

"Because," muttered her Other Self. "You want it to go wrong."

"That's not true!" she said, weakly.

"Ha!" scoffed her Other Self. "You would be happy if this Jemmy Soutar had found gainful employment half way across the world from here."

"No, no, no," she protested, but was only too aware that her negatives sounded singularly unconvincing.

A sharp knock on her bedroom door aroused Meriel from a deep sleep. Sitting up quickly, her pulse pounding in her throat, she called out, "Yes?"

"Are you awake?" Lord Farr asked.

She glanced at her window and found the moon was high in a star-filled sky. "Y-Yes," she answered, trying not to sound sleepy.

"Might I see you?" There was an edge of excitement to his tone that roused her completely, while at the same time it caused her heart to sink.

"I shall be out directly." Reaching for her robe, Meriel slipped it on, hastily, and hurried into the parlor. She had left a candle burning for his return, but it had dwindled to a tiny sputtering flame, and at first she did not see him. Then, she discovered him at the window. He was standing with his back to her, staring into the darkness. "Lord Farr . . ." she began, and paused as turning, he stiffened staring at her in amazement.

"Good God!" he exclaimed.

"Is . . . anything wrong?" she faltered.

"No, nothing," he said, coming toward her. "It's you, your hair, gleaming blue and your face so ivory pale in the moonlight. For the moment, you seemed actually insubstantial." Reaching her, he lifted one of her long tresses, then dropped it quickly, saying a little breathlessly, "It looked like a fall of mist."

She was grateful for the darkness, for she felt her cheeks burning. To cover her confusion, she said, lightly, "If I startled you, my Lord, think what a happy effect I shall have upon Miss Stansfield!"

He nodded, still staring at her. "It will be quite amazing." Concerned, he added, "I hope I did not awaken you."

"No. I was only resting. I have been waiting to hear what happened at the castle. Were you able to find Mr. Soutar?"

"Yes, I found him." He smiled, mischievously.

"Will he help you?"

"Yes, he was game. He said, 'It'll be like old times.'" Lord Farr laughed. "Jemmy was

99

always ripe for mischief. He's not changed. Indeed, he gave me some very good suggestions, regarding timing—fortunately, his services will not be required at the castle on Thursday evening."

"Thursday evening . . . the day after tomorrow?" she questioned weakly. "Is that when my . . . appearance will . . . take place?"

"Yes, Thursday evening. The Duke has played into our hands, as it were."

She valiantly swallowed a lump in her throat. "In what way?"

"Tomorrow night, he and his guests will be going to a ball. On Thursday, he'll be giving a small dinner at home. The banqueting hall adjoins the courtyard and from the courtyard, it is quite easy to see the North Turret. Soon after the Duke has gone into dinner— say between the soup and the fish courses— you will make your appearance. Jemmy will be in the courtyard to spread the alarm. Tomorrow night, we shall take you through the passage."

"You will leave me in it until . . ."

"Leave you in it? Of course not. Do you think I could be so cruel? No, it is necessary for us to gauge the time it will take you to make the ascent. It is a bit steep, I fear, for the turret is high. I think you will want to rest at various points along the way."

"I see . . ." She forced a smile. "You seem to have thought of everything."

"With Jemmy's help." He put his arm around her. "You are not frightened, I hope."

"Frightened?" She shook her head, her blue hair catching the moonlight, and wished his arm would tighten. She wished . . . but dared not frame those particular wishes. "No, of course not," she said, valiantly. "There's nothing to be frightened about."

Lord Farr gave her an approving squeeze and moved away. "Good girl. Of course, there isn't. You'll need to appear only for a few moments—then, you will walk back into the passageway."

"You're sure the Duke will not think of looking into the passageway, himself?"

"As I think I've told you, he was a nervous child, and he's not a particularly brave man. If he sees you, I think he'll be in no condition to reason cogently." Confidently, he continued. "You need not have qualms, Meriel." He let his eyes rest on her for a long moment, adding, perhaps more revealingly than he might have intended, "Since viewing you in the moonlight, my own fears are quite at rest. I am convinced that nothing can go wrong."

Ruthlessly, Meriel quelled the little shiver that went through her at that moment, saying firmly if untruthfully, "Nor have I any qualms, my Lord, none at all, I assure you."

It was cold in the passageway, and as Lord Farr had said more than once during their erratic course upward, it contained considerably more twists than he had remembered. He had also observed that its condition had worsened since the years when he and Jemmy had braved it. At various points during the steep ascent, they had come across piles of masonry, which having fallen from ceiling and walls had left great cavernous gaps. However, as Meriel was discovering, it was quite negotiable if one was careful. Still, she wished that Jemmy Soutar, who was walking ahead of them, would not swing his lantern quite so freely, for it set strange patterns of light to dancing on the shattered walls. Those, coupled with the dank chill of the place, combined to give it an eerie atmosphere, which was proving strangely intimidating. Equally intimidating were the thick spider webs that occasionally stretched across the passage. Fortunately, these were quickly destroyed by the stick Jemmy had had the forethought to bring with him. As she passed between their remaining filaments, Meriel was thankful that Lord Farr had insisted upon this rehearsal. It would have been extremely disquieting to have ventured into the passage for the first time tomorrow night. She came to an abrupt stop, as a shard of stone from the ceiling, evidently dislodged by the vibrations of their steps, fell narrowly missing her head and sending a shower of tiny granite chips down on her face.

While she was blinking them out of her eyes and brushing them from her face, Lord Farr, who had been a few paces behind her, stepped to her side and, setting down his lantern, said anxiously, "I hope none of that went into your eyes."

"They're out now," she assured him.

"Are you positive?"

"Yes, quite. Thank you."

"You're breathing hard," he noted. "I think we must rest again. Jemmy!" he called to the groom, who, apparently unaware of the incident, was still moving doggedly ahead.

"My Lord?"

"Do not go any farther—we will remain here for a few moments. Miss Hathaway is tired."

As the man turned back, Meriel said, "Please, I am not tired. Is it much farther to the Turret?"

"Is it, Jemmy?" Lord Farr asked, as he came up to them.

"It becomes much steeper around the next bend," Jemmy replied. "So I shouldn't think there was much of a way to go." He shook his head. "I thought I knew every inch of this passageway, but it's been a long time since I've been in it."

"It seems a long time since anyone's been in it," Lord Farr observed. "I'd lay a monkey on it—there's not been a soul here since we used it as our hideaway, eh, Jemmy?"

"I'm thinking you'd win your bet, my Lord," Soutar agreed. "Sure his Grace's not put a toe inside."

"Not since the time we dragged him in here as our prisoner of war," Lord Farr spoke, wistfully. As if, Meriel thought with some amusement, he wished he might have his cousin in so ignominious a position again. She was sure of it when he added, "Do you remember how he squealed like a trapped stoat?"

"And told the old Duke on us, later," Jemmy said wryly. "Aye, I do."

"Ah, yes," Lord Farr chuckled. "We were both soundly thrashed, but each time I thought of Rex's face, I'd no regrets, nor had you, Jemmy. We had great times together."

"Yes, we surely did," Jemmy agreed, dutifully, but Meriel thought he sounded disgruntled. Earlier, when he had been presented to her, she had surprised a sullen look on his face. She had also noted a certain puffiness around his eyes and a high flush to his cheeks, which hinted at too many tankards of ale or, possibly, long draughts of "Blue Ruin." She felt a little sorry for him. He was a well-set-up young man and, judging from Lord Farr's affectionate manner toward him, she was sure they had once been very close friends. However, on coming of age, Lord Farr had acquired the control of a large fortune, while Jemmy, still in the service of the noble house of Broxbridge, had risen no higher than Second Coachman. She could imagine his envy and frustration.

Indeed, she thought, more bitterly than usual, she could even share it. Though she was gently bred, her position was close to Jemmy Soutar's. A chasm divided them from the rich Lord Farr, who unthinkingly availed himself of both their services and would, as soon as their usefulness was at an end, forget them —as he must have forgotten Jemmy these many years. She moved restlessly, not wanting to think about it.

"My Lord," she said, a little sharply. "I should like to go on. It's passing close in here. . . . I feel the need of fresh air."

"But of course," he agreed, hastily. "The air is heavy in here and dusty, too. I beg your pardon, Meriel." Motioning to Jemmy, who picked up his lantern, they continued along the passageway which, as they rounded the bend, became not only steeper but narrower and lower, causing the men to keep their heads down. They slowed their steps and, for the next several minutes, all that was heard was the sound of their footfalls on the rough stone floor and their labored breathing as the incline rose sharply.

Moving nearer to Meriel, Lord Farr said, apologetically, "I fear that in the interim between youth and maturity, I forgot that a sally forth was not so much intended as a 'sally back.' I do hope you'll forgive me for this discomfort."

It was amazing, she mused. He had but to drop a kind word in her ear and all her incipient resentment vanished as quickly as morning dew. Now, feeling it incumbent upon her to reassure him, she said, "But I am not in any discomfort. I am finding it quite an adventure."

"Meriel, Meriel," he slipped his arms around her waist. Meriel hoped the shiver that went through her could not be felt by Lord Farr. "I think I am right in declaring that there's not another female like you in all of England."

"Here we are, my Lord." Jemmy called out.

Releasing Meriel, Lord Farr glanced up. "Where . . . I don't see it?"

Jemmy lifted his lantern to reveal a large oblong slab of stone directly overhead. "There it is, my Lord."

"Oh, yes." Lord Farr's eyes lighted. "It seems to me that the opening's on that side."

"Opening?" Meriel stared at the stone. It

appeared to her that it was fixed in its position for all time, but, at a push from Jemmy, it slid back a crack and she felt a gust of cold air against her face.

"Is that the most you can open it?" Lord Farr asked, nervously.

"No . . ." Jemmy pushed again and it slid back easily along the two grooves on either side. Through the opening, it was possible to see a patch of starry sky.

"Good man," Lord Farr approved. "You climb on out and I'll lift Meriel up to you."

A few moments later, the three of them stood on the Turret. It seemed much larger in circumference than it had when Meriel saw it from the hillock. The crenelated top of the structure rose nearly to her chin. "How will anyone be able to see me from here?"

"You'll not stay here," Lord Farr pointed to a raised granite block. "You'll be there, where the look-out was wont to stand. It's also the place where the specter is reputed to appear. Over here"—he walked a few paces to the left—"is the trapdoor, which will give us access into the rest of the castle."

Following him, Meriel found a small, flat, wooden door, fastened with a padlock. "You'll enter this way, then?"

He nodded. "Yes—it's connected with the second floor, and it will let me out in an un-used wing of the Hall. I'll make my way to the chapel. After Jemmy has brought you to the Turret, he will follow the stairs down to the courtyard. . . . When the excitement is at its height, I'll come back here and lock the door. Then, you and I will leave by the sally forth." He looked at Jemmy. "You're sure you'll have no trouble obtaining the key."

"None, my Lord," he answered tonelessly.

"Why have you chosen to wait in the chapel?" Meriel asked curiously.

"I can see most of the courtyard from there." He turned toward Jemmy. "Is anyone likely to see Meriel, if she stands on this block for a moment or two?"

"I shouldn't think so, my Lord."

"Come then, Meriel. Let us see how much of you can be seen."

Obediently she stepped up on the block and gasped; for she found herself looking down on a great sweep of land, diminished by the height of the tower into maplike contours. There were miniature houses and dwarfed trees. There were lines, which were roads and others of moon-brightened water. Above her, stretched a sky filled with legions of stars, commanded by a cold bright orb that wanted only a day before it swelled into a full moon. It was a beautiful and peaceful sight, but she remembered why she was there and, in remembering, thought of the legend—the poor girl brought up to this high tower and pushed to her death.

Terror rose in her as she seemed to feel the hands of the man she had loved, those same hands that had caressed her, turned hard as, inexorably, he pushed her back, back against the wall. She was being lifted . . . she tried to reach for something, but there was nothing to grasp, for she was being held high in the air . . . he was so strong, this man, who had been her lover. . . . She had never been any

match for his strength. . . . she had been unable to defend herself against his ruthless passion . . . and he had made her love him.

"Meriel," Lord Farr said. "Do you suppose you might take off your turban? I should
like to see your hair in the moonlight."

For a moment, she looked at him blankly,
caught in the grip of her own imagination—
or had it been her imagination? She had an
odd sense of invasion, as if for a few moments
another entity had dwelt within her. She gave
herself a little shake. She was not a forsaken
maiden; she was here to play a part. Obediently, she removed her headdress.

"Lud!" Jemmy took an involuntary step
backward, his eyes wide. "Lud!" he repeated
in a shaky whisper. "I'm glad I know she's
flesh and blood."

Lord Farr walked about the Turret survey-
ing her from one angle and then another.
She did, indeed, look like Lady Blue. "Yes,"
he said, finally, "it's even more effective than
I imagined it would be. It should cause quite
a stir in the household."

"That it will," Jemmy agreed. "I'm thinking there'll be more than one case of vapors
belowstairs."

"And above them as well." Lord Farr
laughed.

"Meriel forced a smile. "I do hope so, my
Lord."

He looked at her for a long moment, then
bowed deeply. "I thank you, my Lady Blue."

Meriel had never known a day to pass so

slowly. Yet, now, with her hooded cloak hiding her flowing azure hair and the diaphanous blue gauze robe, which Lord Farr told her answered to the descriptions of Lady Blue's garments, she thought that the time had passed all too quickly. Not only the hours, but the days. Now, finally, the night, for which they had traveled halfway across England was upon them. In a matter of minutes, she would be hearing Jemmy's summoning whistle and then, in another two hours, she would be back in her chamber again—her task at an end. On the morrow, they would be bound for Bath—a few more days, and then it would be farewell to Neville Farr . . . farewell, forever.

"Oh," she murmured to herself, "if he could have stayed with me . . . just for tonight. I will be all alone on the Turret."

"Naturally." Her Other Self began.

"Hush! I'll not listen to you."

Her objections were futile. "Naturally," continued her Other Self, "he will want to witness the immediate reaction to his lady specter. I think he'll not be disappointed. Miss Stansfield will come dashing into the courtyard . . . and if there's a man nearby, she'll probably faint into his arms. Lady Susan says it's one of her favorite ploys."

Meriel smiled wryly. She hoped that the possible spectacle of Miss Stansfield's practiced swoon would not prove too much for Lord Farr's sensibilities. If he were to come to her aid . . . Meriel tensed. Had she heard a whistle? Moving closer to the window, she stood listening intently and heard it again.

Clutching her cloak about her, she hurried into the parlor and sped down into the darkness to meet Jemmy Soutar.

The immense, forbidding castle was very close, and the small squares of light shining through the windows seemed like so many eyes piercing the darkness. Argus eyes, she thought gloomily, which would soon fasten upon her. She and Jemmy rode up the trail that wound in and out of the small clumps of scraggly bushes and stunted trees growing out of the rocky soil at the base of the rise. On the previous evening, she had barely noticed the ugliness of the terrain, but then Lord Farr had been at her side. She could still picture his tall, muscular body, silhouetted in the moonlight, and once again, she fervently wished for his company.

She darted a little glance at Jemmy. Certainly, he presented a sorry contrast as he sat slumped in his saddle. Much to her distress, she'd found him in a very strange mood, alternating between sullenness and uncontrollable laughter. Judging from the strong whiff of spirits she'd smelled on his breath when he had helped her mount, she feared that he was more than half-foxed. Obviously, he had gone to the tavern, after he brought them the key to the Turret door. That might be the reason for the slowness of their pace.

"Should we not hurry?" She asked, urgently leaning forward.

"We'll be there in good time, Lady Blue. . . . We'll be there in good time."

"But we're going so slowly." She was at a

loss. How could anyone reason with a man in this condition?"

"Then we'll go faster! Faster!" Jemmy spurred his horse forward. "Come on, Lady Blue! Faster!" Laughing crazily, he galloped recklessly ahead.

Meriel felt a little thrill of fear, wondering why he had drunk so much at so crucial a moment. She remembered her earlier impressions of him. Was this a way of expressing his resentment? She wished she had mentioned her observations to Lord Farr. Suppose Jemmy failed them? He was certainly in no condition to lead her through the passageway.

"Come on!" Jemmy called from the edge of the woods. The entrance to the passage was directly ahead, but as she looked he disappeared amongst the trees. With a frightened gasp, Meriel urged her horse into a gallop, more than half afraid she might not be able to locate him.

However, once she had entered the grove, he stepped forward holding up a lantern, his face looking crazed and eerie in the light. Ignoring her fears and without waiting for his help, she dismounted hastily. He took the reins silently and with much fumbling, tied the horse to a tree not far from where he had tethered his own mount. "Come."

Raising his lantern, Jemmy led the way to the massive boulder. She watched, tension mounting, wondering if, in his drunken state, he would be able to find the point where the stone swung back. Fortunately, he found it immediately. The boulder shifted and turned under the pressure of his hand. Lifting the lantern he lighted her way inside. "I better go ahead," he muttered, stepping around her and starting to walk quickly.

"Please . . . not so fast," she begged.

"I thought you were in a hurry," he said, with another of his uncontrolled laughs.

"I might not be able to keep up with you."

"All right, I'll go slower." He moved forward at a snail's pace, and she had the feeling he was deliberately mocking her, but she did not dare complain. Finally, he fell into a normal rate of speed and she breathed more easily, hoping fervently that she would have no more trouble with him.

They had penetrated some distance into the dark passageway when she heard a crash behind her. Meriel stiffened, for she heard another sound—footsteps? She halted, listening, and then, she thought she heard more steps. With a gasp, she moved forward quickly. "Jemmy . . ."

"Wha'sit?" he demanded, his voice more slurred than before.

"I . . . think I heard footsteps. There might be someone b-back of us, following us."

He stood still, listening 'I don' hear anythin'." He shook his head.

"No, not at present, but I did hear . . ."

"Come along." His laughter reverberated through the tunnel. "Couldn't be anyone . . . nobody knows 'bout this place ceptin' his damned, stiff-necked, lily-livered Grace 'n' his Lordship . . . lil' Neville Farr. . . ." He looked at her owlishly, then put his hand heavily on her shoulder. "Do anythin' for Master Neville,

Miss, anythin'. We're friends. Jemmy, the stable boy'n' Neville, the Earl. We're friends. Can you believe that?"

"Please, hush. I tell you . . . I heard . . ."

"An' I tell you, lil' blue lady . . . it's your imag-imagination. Unless you heard a ghost, but you couldn't hear a ghost—*you're* the ghost."

"Oh, please," she begged, "shine the lantern back of us." She tried to take it from him. "Or I shall do it."

"No." He held it above her, far out of her reach. "We mus' go ahead, we'll be late'n' it'll be too late'n' his Grace'll 've finished swillin' down his drink an' gulpin' his food'n' all will be spoilt." An ugly look crossed his face. "Don' wan' it to be spoilt . . . wan' to see his Grace scared like he was when we brought him in here. . . . Should've heard him yell. Wish I could hear him yell, now. . . . Maybe I will'n' be paid for it, too. Master Neville'll pay me. Master Neville's my good friend'n' he's offered me good money. Maybe I'll use it to buy me a passage to Australia'n' become rich. Rich Jemmy Soutar wi' a fine gold watch'n' more fine gold to jingle in my pockets. . . ." His laugh, edged with bitterness, rang through the passageway. Then, he went on ahead, walking unsteadily.

Anger at his drunkenness and her dependency upon him, raged through Meriel. Amazingly, she found herself angry at Lord Farr as well. How could he have failed to see that Jemmy Soutar had all the marks of a drunkard about him? She knew why. He could see nothing besides the unfolding of his scheme to win the lovely Miss Stansfield. She sighed and then she tensed.

The darkness had closed in on her. She moved forward and then stopped; she heard footsteps. She could not tell whether they were in back of her or in front. In that moment, she stopped breathing, then a light was in her eyes.

"Come on," Jemmy Soutar said, querulously.

By the time the passageway turned steep and narrow, Meriel was inclined to agree with Jemmy that she had imagined the footsteps, for she did not hear them again. Finally, they reached the slab of stone, and though he was much winded and more unsteady than ever, Jemmy, managed to thrust it back. Reaching up, he set the lantern on the Turret floor, and with a coarse attempt at gallantry, he beckoned to her. "You first, lil' Lady Blue."

"Shall I climb up?" she asked as she came to him.

"No, I'll put ye there." Before she knew quite what he was about, he'd seized her around the hips and given her a hefty boost that sent her sprawling through the cavity, falling full length on the rough stones, barking shins and scraping her hands.

Biting back a cry of indignation, she clambered to her feet in time to hear a groan and a thud. Frightened, she moved to the edge of the opening, staring downward. She did not see him. "Jemmy?" she whispered. "Are you hurt?"

There was a moment of silence, then a

whisper. "No, I be all right. Stand out of the way."

As she obeyed, he put his two hands on the edge of the aperture and hoisted himself up quickly. Startled Meriel saw a thin, spidery, black-clad body and a gaunt sallow face, barred by heavy black brows and, horror of horrors, a white filmy eye. With a terrified gasp, she fled, but was halted by the side of the Turret. Quickly, he sprang to her side, his hand raised menacingly. Instinctively, she tried to dodge the blow, but was unable to avoid it. His fist descended. There was an instant of pain, then she knew nothing more.

# (6)

Meriel was being jounced from side to side. It was most uncomfortable, for her head ached dreadfully. Furthermore, she was terribly confused. It was another moment before she realized that she was on a horse, and there was a slow steady beat beneath her ear, a heart beat! She was lying against someone's chest, held very firmly in two strong arms. She had an instant's terrifying memory of a menacing face and that disfigured white eye. With a little gasp, she tried to pull away, and the horse, startled by her sudden movement, shied.

"Steady, boy . . . steady" The animal, pulled in by the reins, quieted down.

She knew that voice! "L-Lord F-Farr," she breathed. "Why . . . w-what . . ?"

"Shhhh," he said, very gently. "You must not try to talk, Meriel."

"But how . . . but why?"

"Shhhhh," he cautioned again. "Close your eyes, my dear, and don't move."

His warning came a second too late, for she had turned her head quickly, and with the movement had come a throbbing pain and an accompanying faintness. With a little moan, she felt herself falling into darkness once more.

When she awakened again, the jouncing had mercifully stopped and she was in her bed at the inn. A cool wet cloth was across her brow. Again she was confused, for it was still dark, but she could see an edging of sunlight around the curtains at her window. She wondered that the hours of the night had passed so quickly. She tried to sit up but the room swam about her in a most disconcerting manner. There was nothing for it but to lie still. Then, out of the corner of her eye, she was aware of a movement. A chair creaked and was pushed back, then Lord Farr bent over her, looking at her anxiously. "Meriel, how are you feeling?"

"I . . . what happened after . . ." She tried to raise herself.

"No," he said gently, pressing her back against her pillows. "Do you want water or . . ."

"N-No," she started to say, then discovered that her mouth was very dry. "A . . . little water," she murmured.

He moved back and she heard the sound of water being poured into a glass. Coming to the bed, he slid his arm beneath her shoulders, raising her very carefully, as he tipped the glass toward her lips. Comforted by his strong arm, she drank gratefully. She noticed even in that dim light, that he looked pale, tired, and considerably disheveled. His hair was rumpled, there was a dark stubble of beard on his cheeks, his garments were sadly creased and his cravat untied. Meeting his eyes, she found them full of concern and of an expression she could not quite interpret.

"Have you had enough?"

"Yes." she smiled faintly. "I do thank you."

He frowned. "You've nothing to thank me for, my poor girl." Setting the glass down on the table near the bed, he put his hand on the cloth that covered her forehead. "This has grown dry. I'll put more water on it."

As he took it off, she turned her head slightly and saw a chair pulled near the night table. A blanket was thrown negligently over it and a pillow lay on the floor. With a stab of amazement, she realized that he must have been sitting by her bedside all night.

She puzzled over that, then, her confusion began to fade and a vivid image of the man with the white eye came to her. She remembered the blow—but more than that, she remembered Jemmy.

"My Lord!" she gasped.

He was at her side in an instant. "Are you in pain?"

"No," she said, quickly. "I did but wonder about poor Jemmy. . . . What happened to him . . . the man with the eye must have hurt him, too."

"The . . . eye?" Lord Farr repeated.

"A . . . white eye. I saw it; as he came out of the passage. But Jemmy? What of Jemmy?"

Lord Farr gave her a rueful look, but did not answer immediately. Stepping away from her, he fetched the cloth, laying it gently over her forehead. "You must not think of these things now; rest and sleep. We shall talk later."

"No," she protested in stronger tones. "Please tell me!" With a little frightened gasp, she whispered, "He . . . he has not been slain?"

"No, no," Lord Farr assured her. "He, too, was struck down, but he has a hard head. A hard head and a loose tongue," he sighed. "But it's not Jemmy I blame for all that has occurred. The fault was mine, entirely mine." His second sigh was so deep as to border on a groan. His voice actually trembled as he said, "Oh, Meriel, my poor Meriel, was there ever such a coil and for nothing!" Shaking his head, he added explosively, "I must have been mad . . . utterly mad!"

Meriel moved restively, wishing her head did not throb with every effort she made to raise if from her pillows. She had an absurd longing to slip from the bed and put her arms around Neville Farr, for he seemed much in need of comfort. She had never known him to be so cast down. His habitual ebullience had vanished and with it had gone the impetuous boyish quality that had so often appeared during their travels. He seemed to have gained several years in one night. She said compassionately, "Please, my Lord, do tell me what happened?"

"Very well," he assented, reluctantly. Pulling his chair closer to the bed, he sat down and, after a moment, he began to speak. Though there were long pauses and times when he seemed to have difficulty continuing, the story emerged clearly.

"There was a moment," he told her, ruefully, "when I did not think I could get into the castle at all—for it was very difficult to open the Turret door; finally I succeeded."

"Then . . ." she prompted.

He had gone down the winding stairs to the second floor, then through another unused passageway to the chapel. From its windows, he could command a view of the entire courtyard and better yet, he could see into the Banquet Hall, for the draperies had not been drawn. Through four tall arched windows, he saw portions of the long table, decorated for the occasion with garlands of spring flowers.

He had a certain amount of time to wait before the guests arrived. Finally, they came in and were ceremoniously seated by footmen in ducal livery. Though he could not see all the company, he did find that Lady Stansfield was placed to the right of her host. Lord Farr had a very good view of the Incomparable, who looked magnificent in rose silk. As the feasting began, he could see her talking animatedly with the Marquess of Camberwell, an elderly peer of fifty-odd years, who, nevertheless, seemed as infatuated with the Beauty as a man of half his years. Indeed, he had surprised a deep frown on His Grace's sallow countenance and had been sourly amused to find his cousin in much the same position as himself. His amusement had increased as he thought of the unpleasant surprise in store for the lovely Beatrix. It would, he had thought savagely, wipe the smile from her beautiful mouth. Furthermore, due to Lady Blue's imminent arrival, it would effectively separate her from the amorous Marquess, whose attentions, Meriel guessed, Neville resented quite as hotly as must his cousin.

He had half expected that the sighting of the apparition would have taken place after the fish course, but since it had not, he expected it would happen during the game course. However, somewhat to his surprise, the game was devoured in peace, as were the following courses. Footmen were clearing the table for dessert and he, caught between anger and worry, was wondering if he should not return to the Turret when, to his considerable relief, a maidservant came screaming into the courtyard. He moved to the chapel door, and opened it a crack. He was expecting her to look up at the Turret, and he also expected to see Jemmy close behind her. Instead, he heard the girl blubbering hysterically about a man in black with a gleaming diamond necklace in his hand, whom she had seen moving stealthily into an upstairs chamber. Upon being sighted, he had darted away, vanishing into thin air!

Lord Farr had been confused by this tale, and his suspicions had been aroused. Had Jemmy played him false? Why had Meriel not made her appearance? That she had not, suddenly seemed a matter for very great concern. He wanted to go back up to the second floor and return to the Turret, but now the servants were alerted, and he was afraid he would be seen.

Instead, he'd slipped hastily from the chapel and through the gardens to a place that would bring him outside the walls. Then, he had gone to the passageway just in time to see a dark shape dart past him and disappear among the trees. In another moment, he'd heard the sound of hooves, and, though he had a very good idea that he had seen the escape of the thief, he could give it little thought, for his fears sent him plunging into darkness of the sally forth.

Staying near to the wall, he'd groped his way up the incline; stumbling occasionally and falling once or twice. Finally he'd arrived at the entrance to the Turret. There he had nearly fallen over a recumbent form. For a moment, he feared it might be Meriel, but in the light from the lantern, which yet remained close to the entrance of the passage, he saw that it was Jemmy, who was showing signs of returning to consciousness. He had then scrambled to the top of the Turret. At first, he had not seen Meriel—then, he found her lying against the wall.

At this point in his narrative, he paused to say, in horrified accents, "I . . . thought at first that you were dead." Swallowing convulsively, his eyes full of remembered fear, he continued, "But, then, I found you were breathing."

His first impulse had been to seek aid within the castle, but common sense intervened. It would have required too many explanations and, possibly, his own presence would have aroused suspicion. "Yet, I did not care so much for myself, I could have explained what had happened—but you would have been hopelessly compromised. I could not add that to all my other follies." Giving her a brooding look, he continued, "Consequently, I became an accomplice of the thief, for I locked the Turret door, thus obliterating all evidence of his method of entry."

"Oh!" Meriel protested. "You should not have!"

"No matter," he interrupted, roughly. "I was already an accomplice, rendered so by my own lack of foresight and of observation, as well as by the very nature of my so-called prank. He ran his hands through his hair. "Good God, was there ever so ill-judged an action, so puerile a scheme?"

"My Lord," Meriel protested, "surely you cannot blame yourself for what happened. Certainly, you could not know that a thief was lurking in the vicinity?"

He gave a short, mirthless laugh. " 'Lurking in the vicinity?' " he said, mockingly. "You believe it was all happenstance? It's a comforting theory, but, unfortunately, I cannot be absolved so easily. There is another explanation."

Meeting his somber eyes, she faltered, "Another . . . What can it be?"

"Jemmy."

"Jemmy? Surely, he was not in league with the thief?"

"No, not in league. I'll tell you what happened."

She could have guessed it, she thought. She was not even surprised when he explained that Jemmy, regaining his senses, had told him how, after leaving them on Wednesday evening, he had gone to a nearby tavern and met a friend there. As was his wont, he'd drunk deeply. Some time in the course of a long night, he had a dim memory of having confided the whole scheme. They had considered it a capital joke, but there must have been one, who, unbeknownst to them, had listened and made his plans accordingly. The thief had waited in the woods for Jemmy and Meriel to arrive and followed them into the passageway.

She had gasped at this, saying quickly, "Yes, I heard a noise, footsteps, I thought. But Jemmy . . ." She paused, confused, not wanting to mention his condition.

"Jemmy was three-parts drunk," Lord Farr said, harshly, "Yes, he told me that, too. If I'd used half my intelligence, I would never have involved him in this scheme. I see now that he's sadly changed from the lad I knew. I should have noticed it at once, but I concentrated so on my own pursuits, that I did not take his feelings into account; his feelings and frustrations, poor fellow.

"As a boy, he was ambitious. We used to talk about joining the army together—of even going across the seas to Australia. But, of course, I forgot all about these fancies when I grew older. As for Jemmy, he had a sick mother and three younger sisters to support. His mother died last year and the girls have all gone into service. Life's been difficult for him.

My cousin's not an easy master and, unfortunately, he has a long memory. It must have pleased him to keep Jemmy in his place, as it were. I cannot condemn his drinking. God knows, there's little else for him to do save marry and raise a passel of needy brats."

Listening to him, she was surprised. It was evident to her that after his return to the inn, he'd spent the ensuing hours in deep reflection. Out of this had come not only insight but a new maturity. It was that, she thought, which made him appear older. She said, "Yes, it must have been very hard for him. I sensed he was unhappy."

There was a wry twist to his mouth as he said, heavily, "You, Meriel, are gifted with all the perception that I lack."

"I cannot believe that, my Lord," she said, gently. "I hope Jemmy did not sustain any serious injuries."

"No," he replied, "but he was most dreadfully castdown. I fear I did not offer him comfort enough, for I was so concerned in getting you out of the castle and back to the inn. He was of great help, for in spite of his own aching head, he insisted on lighting us through the passageway."

"Oh, that was brave of him!"

"Very brave," Lord Farr answered. "I mean to see that he's rewarded for it."

"Perhaps, he can yet go to Australia."

"I will see to it. And believe me—I will make it up to you for all you've suffered, my dear. At least, I shall try for I cannot think there is any way that I can succeed.—"

"Please"—she raised a protesting hand—

"I'll not allow you to blame yourself for what happened. It was not your fault. Under other circumstances, I am sure it would have worked out quite as you expected. I am only sorry that I was not able to make my appearance." She managed a laugh. "Indeed, I think, I should have enjoyed watching their reactions."

Her statement elicited no answering smile from him. "I hope you'll not mention that foolery to me again," he said, chokingly. "If you but knew how I felt when I saw you lying there so still. Then . . . to . . . to feel the wetness on my hand . . ."

"Wetness?" she repeated, staring at him.

"You must have struck the back of your head when you fell, for there is a deep welt, which was still bleeding when I found you. It's a wonder your skull was not cracked."

"But it was not," she reminded him. "Indeed my head does not ache so much now. I am feeling much better."

He looked at her suspiciously. "Are you? Or are you only trying to make light of it, because that must ever be your way?"

"It is the truth," she insisted. "A day of rest, and I am sure I shall feel quite the thing again."

He rose. "Yes, you must rest. We've talked far too long."

"And you, my Lord," she said quickly. "you, too, must rest. I fear you've had little sleep."

"Enough," he said gratingly. "I beg you'll not concern yourself over my comfort or the lack of it. I am well enough." Moving nearer, he touched her hair caressingly. Then, quickly, almost before she knew what was happening, he bent to press a kiss upon her lips. "Sleep well, my dear," he said huskily, striding from the room, and closing the door softly behind him.

Dazed, she put a finger to her lips, wondering if she had not imagined his kiss. It had been so swift and so gentle; it should not have left her feeling limp, nor set her heart to pounding, or activated a host of other sensations at various points all over her body. It took some time before she could gather her scattered senses together and think about it calmly and practically. When, at last, she did, she regained her equilibrium with regrettable ease.

Kisses, she thought dispassionately, came in several categories. There were the burning, passionate sort, which he had found described in the romantic novels her father had so derided. Then, there were the chaste, affectionate kisses the more restrained authors preferred. There were kisses of friendship and kisses of apology and, though she would as lief not acknowledge it, it was to this latter category that she could allocate Lord Farr's kiss.

"For surely," she whispered to herself, "he cannot have forgotten Miss Stansfield."

She had a sudden vivid memory of Miss Stansfield in her rose silk gown. For a moment, she was confused. She had seen the Incomparable but once and then she had been clad in brown, a stylish brown walking dress, extremely becoming, but neither rose-colored nor silk. A long shuddering sigh escaped her as she remembered from whence or rather from whom, she had had that specific description. It had not been her memory that had conjured it up, but Lord Farr's, whose words rendered it vivid in her mind. Implicit in those same words had been pain—his pain and sense of loss.

She shook her head, a movement she immediately regretted, since it set a covey of twinges to skittering back and forth across her temples. Still, she pursued her thoughts, which decried the fate that had kept her from making her appearance. Even though it might have sent Miss Stansfield into his arms, it would have kept him from all the shame and suffering that were now his portion. If only he were not so determined to blame himself. It was *not* his fault, however much he insisted it was!

He could not have known of Jemmy Soutar's resentment, and it had been that which lay at the root of the situation. Resentment had turned him into a drunkard and a deeper resentment had loosened his tongue. She was sure of that, sure that unconsciously, he had wanted to reveal the plan and keep Lord Farr from winning his beloved. She wished she might present this explanation to Lord Farr, for it might serve to ease the weight of the guilt he had insisted upon assuming. But she knew it would be useless. It would not help him to know that particular truth—if truth it were and not merely a supposition on her part. It would only hurt Jemmy and, certainly, it could have no effect upon the situation at Broxbridge Hall. Miss Stansfield, well-shielded from the ghostly meanderings of

Lady Blue, would remain at the castle, flirting happily with the Marquess of Camberwell and, perhaps, yielding eventually to the Duke's blandishments.

Meriel felt a dull ache in the region of her heart and knew it had nothing to do with the hurts the thief had inflicted upon her. These would heal, but there was no balm for an agony that came from the soul. She thought of Lord Farr's kiss, compounded from equal parts of kindness and compassion. For a wild moment, she wished she might have convinced herself that it really stemmed from love, but, she grimaced, fortunately she was far too sensible for that. Being so utterly sensible, it took her an hour to stem the tears that flowed down her cheeks, and in another forty minutes, she had, sensibly, fallen into a fitful slumber.

# (7)

The sun was high in a cloudless sky. In the distance, the river gleamed, bright blue patterned with gold. Small boats bobbed up and down, and a flock of swallows swooped overhead. Meriel, clad once more in her widow's weeds, had been feeling quite as somber as her garments indicated, until, tempted by the sunshine, she'd gone to the window.

Gazing out, she could not restrain a surge of joy at the serene beauty spread before her. In her head was a stanza from Herbert, "Sweet spring, full of sweet days and roses . . ." She had not spied any roses, as yet, but surely this was a sweet spring day. Furthermore, she could drink in its beauty without a throbbing at her temples.

Despite a certain depression, she felt better after her long sleep of yesterday and this morning. She'd had awakened to find that all traces of her pain and dizziness had vanished. Yet, thinking of her quick recovery, her earlier unhappiness returned, for, naturally, she had been quick to convey the information concerning her improved state of health to Lord Farr. He had received it in a silence, which he broke a few moments later, to say heavily, "Then . . . on the morrow, we must leave for Bath."

She knew what was troubling him. The news of the robbery at the castle had spread quickly. Toward evening of the previous day, Lord Farr had learned from the landlord of the inn, that Miss Stansfield and her mother had lost valuable jewelry. The Duke had been robbed of some gold fobs and a black pearl cravat pin. Meriel knew that Lord Farr, holding himself responsible for the crime, longed to make reparations to the victims and to confess the whole to his cousin. Instead, because of her reputation, he was leaving without a word.

Earlier that morning, she had dared to argue with him. "Why will you not tell him the whole story. It would be better than for you to suffer!"

"No!" He had interrupted firmly. "I could not implicate you, Meriel."

"But he'd not need to know that I am . . . I," she'd said.

"But, eventually, he would know," he had replied, adding bitterly, "You seem to forget, Meriel, that I have a well-earned reputation for tomfoolery. The story would leak out and my Aunt Lithwaite would be only too pleased to impart her knowledge of your blue hair to the Polite World. It would be something you could not live down. No, Rex must remain in ignorance, and I shall endeavor to make amends in secret."

"But . . ." she'd started to protest.

He'd lifted an impatient hand. "Pray, let us not mention this again, Meriel," he had said, firmly.

He would not mention it again, she was sure of that. However, during the three days it might take before they arrived in Bath, his guilt and the loss of Miss Stansfield would be preying on his mind, which meant that she dared not even hope for a glimpse of the man whose companionship she had found so exhilarating during the earlier stages of their journey. The change she had noted yesterday morning had persisted. He remained moody, preoccupied, and given to long periods of silence. In fact, aside from administering to her needs, as he had continued to do throughout the late afternoon and evening, he had little to say to her outside of punctilious inquiries concerning her comfort. Though she was convinced that his attitude was based mainly on his distress over the untoward consequences of his prank, she felt some of it might also stem from the kiss. Perhaps he feared that she might have put the wrong construction upon something he had meant as a merely friendly gesture, for though he had remained unfailingly courteous, his manner had been definitely distant.

There was a tap at her door. She started

and hurried to open it. Lord Farr, looking so immaculate and handsome as to set her heart to beating overfast, stood outside. He gave her a brief, cold smile. "It is a fine day and you have been inside far too long. I think it would be well if you came for a little drive with me."

She hesitated. Any pleasure that she might have taken at his invitation was negated by the way he had voiced it. In fact, noting his chill glance, she wondered if he really saw her at all. It was on the tip of her tongue to plead a return of her weakness, but instead, she could not keep herself from saying, with an eagerness she would have subdued, "I should enjoy that very much, my Lord."

Throwing a quick nervous glance over his shoulder at the parlor, he stepped into her room. Closing the door, he stood against it, saying sharply, "I am your *brother*, Meriel. Kindly address me as such in private as well as in company, else you will surely forget. I'd not have you compromise yourself any more than is necessary."

She flushed at his harsh tone. "Yes, Ulric . . . I did forget. I am sorry."

"Do not always be sorry!" he snapped. Then, looking ashamed, he said in a softer voice, "I beg your pardon, Meriel. I am an ill-tempered brute. I . . ."

"Please," she interrupted. "I do understand."

A brief smile flickered in his eyes, as taking her hand, he lifted it to his lips, saying, "You are far too patient with me, my dear."

She pulled her hand away quickly, unwilling to bear the sweet agony of his touch. Then, seeing his startled expression, she said, hastily, "If . . . if we're to keep up our pretense throughout the following days, we must, as you dictated, maintain it in and out of company. I am without personal experience of brothers, but from what I have observed of the breed, they are slow, I think, to kiss their sisters' hands."

It was his turn to redden. "I think you are right. For though as you know, I have no sisters, those of my friends who are so blessed are not much given to such gestures." A trace of his old mischievous smile quirked the corners of his mouth. "In the future, I think I must bite your hand rather than kiss it." Then, suddenly he frowned and said coldly, "But come—enough of such nonsense. The chaise is below."

At Lord Farr's request, the coachman did not turn his horses toward High Street, but took, instead, the byways leading through the end of the village farthest from the castle. It was a very pretty route, for at one point they rambled over a little stone bridge that spanned a stream made green by the reflection of tall elms and oaks and by the drooping branches of a graceful willow. Lily pads lay on its surface and between them floated a bevy of white swans. Later, they passed some charming cottages with thick thatched roofs and timbered sides. Then, in the distance, she saw the walls of the ruined cloister, brightened by green vines and wild roses.

At the beginning of their drive, she had tried to bring these beauties to his attention, but her rhapsodies had fallen into a pool of silence, and giving him a quick look, she had found him sitting glumly in his corner, indifferent to the passing scenery. Consequently, she kept her pleasure at a remarkably well-preserved Roman arch to herself, nor did she mention the fields of wildflowers with their fluttering complement of vividly colored butterflies. Then, on rounding a bend, she saw a group of bright tents and in the same moment, heard the familiar strains of a brass band. Unthinkingly, she clutched Lord Farr's arm, saying excitedly, "The circus . . . they . . . they've caught up with us!"

Evidently startled out of his mood of dark introspection, he stared down at her dazedly. "What?" he demanded.

She removed her hand quickly, but still she said, "Do you not hear? Look out the window. There's a circus over there. It must be the same one we visited. Do you think we might go again? The Gypsy, I should like to see her. She predicted,"—suddenly the words died on Meriel's lips, as she had recalled Madame Astra's prophecy: "pain and bloodshed."

A frown lingered in his eyes. "I hardly think . . ." he began, then, looking at her, he shrugged. "Well, perhaps we might walk through. There's little likelihood of encountering my cousin and his guests."

"Oh, please, I'd not have you go . . ." she began.

Ignoring her, he signaled the coachman, giving his instructions in so lackluster a tone that once more, she was about to beg that they drive on. But even as she opened her mouth, she changed her mind. There was a possibility that once they were in the lively purlieus of the fairgrounds, Lord Farr's flagging spirits might receive a lift, especially if she could maneuver him back to the tent of the Great Khan. Consequently, she clamped her teeth together, resolutely imprisoning her ready tongue.

The coachman let them out close to the section of the fair alotted to the Oddities. As usual, it was extremely crowded as wide-eyed men and women from the neighboring farms alternately laughed and shuddered as they peered at the Two-Headed Calf and at the incredible Seven-Foot Giant, as he balanced a midget in one mighty palm. They laughed uneasily as the India-Rubber Man pulled out great lengths of skin from his face and arms. They blanched at the human skeleton's stick-like extremities. As before, however, the majority of the exhibits were represented mainly by the highly-colored posters that festooned the tents, and Meriel was pleased to see that Lord Farr lingered and even smiled at a horrendous rendering of a snake-like creature with a human head billed as: THE ONE AND ONLY PYTHON MAN: *a cross between snake and man, found in the dark depths of the Peruvian jungles. Ferocious and dangerous, he combines the amazing strength of a boa constrictor with the deadly venom of a cobra.*

"Lord, I should like to pit him against Gentleman Jackson," he said, "but I fear they'd cry foul."

"Have you sparred with him?" Meriel asked interestedly.

"A few rounds," he said. "Ah," his eyes lighted, "what have we here?"

They had strolled to another tent, which from its poster was supposedly offering asylum to "THE HORRID, HORRENDOUS HALF-MAN, HALF-APE: *captured in darkest Africa. The sole specimen of its breed ever to be found in captivity!!!* The accompanying picture, labeled HARRY, THE HAIRY, showed a strange being, completely covered with long black hair. Sharp white fangs curved over its lips, its face was contorted into a bestial snarl, and in its gigantic arms it was carrying a captive maiden.

"Now that, my dear Meriel," Lord Farr said, "is what I should call a 'warm embrace.'"

She laughed delightedly. As she had hoped, his spirits had been restored. There was a twinkle in his eyes and he was obviously enjoying himself. She said, "Imagine, I might find a niche here, myself. They could bill me as BERTHA, THE BLUE-HEADED WOMAN!" The minute she had spoken, she would have given much to unsay those heedless words, for the laughter fled from his eyes and she received a look so stricken that she was actually frightened. "I didn't mean . . . I was only . . ." she stuttered.

"Come, you wanted to see the Gypsy," he said, shortly. "Let's try to find her and have done."

"I didn't mean . . ." she began, but he was not listening to her. He was striding ahead so quickly that it was difficult to keep up with him. Bitterly chiding herself for her lack of tact in reminding him of the recent debacle, she tried to make her way through the dense

137

crowds. It was difficult, for almost directly overhead a rope-dancer was precariously balancing himself on a length of wire stretched between two large poles. Masses of people had stopped to watch. Then, suddenly, Lord Farr halted and waited for her, saying curtly, "Have I not told you that we must stay together. It's easy to lose your way in these multitudes." He looked about him distastefully.

Inadvertently, she followed his glance, saying, "If you would prefer to leave, I . . ." Then she tensed, for she'd glimpsed a thin, spidery figure garbed in black, who was standing just beyond them. Unlike those who were gawking at the tightrope, he had no eyes for the performer's plight. Instead, he was looking about him furtively, out of his one good eye. Even before she saw the other eye, she knew it would be white. There was no mistaking that form or those incongruously heavy brows. Vaguely, she heard Lord Farr speaking, but she paid no heed. Hardly aware of her own actions, she darted forward, and in another instant, she had reached the thief, and grabbing his coat, she clung to him with all her strength.

" 'Ere!" He whirled about, staring down at her in a fury. "Wot're ye about?"

"Meriel!" Lord Farr hurried to her side, looking at her incredulously. "What?"

"It's him . . . the . . . man with the eye . . . the white eye, the thief . . ." she shrilled, and scarcely had the words left her mouth than she felt a blow to her stomach that sent her reeling back in a haze of pain. Clutching her body, she fell gasping to the ground, as above her, with a cry of rage, Lord Farr sprang on her assailant and bore him to the ground. Above them, the crowds, excited by the scuffle made a great circle around the two men.

Arms and legs flailing, increasing his resemblance to a great black spider, the thief, spewing out a string of oaths, tried to extricate himself from his antagonist's hard grip. It was apparent to the excited onlookers that he possessed a wiry strength surprising for one so slight. For a moment, it seemed as if he might escape, as wrenching himself free, he leaped away preparatory to diving through the mass of people. As a group of them nervously shrank back, Lord Farr caught the thief's ankle, sending him sprawling once again. With a snarl like that of a mad dog, the man made a lightning move with his hand.

Meriel, spent and winded, saw a flash of steel in the sunlight and gasped a warning, "Knife! He's got a knife!" She was echoed by those who had seen the weapon descend from arm to hand, snaking into Lord Farr's shoulder only to be pulled out again as the thief aimed his weapon at his enemy's heart, but in that moment, Lord Farr, seemingly unaware of his injury, drove his fist against the man's narrow face, stunning him.

Two burly farmers stepped in to seize the thief, as another man elbowed his way through the crowds, as someone screamed, "Constable! Fetch the constable!"

The third man came forward saying in harsh tones of authority, "I am the Constable. What has happened here?" Glancing at the prostrate thief, he rasped, "Who is this man?"

"He . . . he . . ." Meriel managed to stagger to her feet. "He's the thief who . . . robbed my Lord Farr's cousin, the . . . the Duke of Broxbridge."

A wind-like whisper ran through the crowd, and she heard the name "Broxbridge" repeated, while the constable, his eyes narrowing, stared at her. "How would you know that, Miss?"

"I saw him . . ." Her words ended abruptly in a cry of horror as Lord Farr, paling, suddenly fell backward in a dead faint.

"N-Neville." Meriel fell on her knees beside him, easing his body into her arms and cradling his head against her breast. "A physician . . . a physician! Please fetch a physician," she begged, distractedly, pressing her hand against Lord Farr's shoulder in a vain attempt to staunch the blood that was seeping from his wound.

"A physician . . . a physician . . ." echoed the people around them in a medley of cries, whispers, and mutterings, which rendered the request almost unintelligible, while in that same moment the thief, suddenly recovering consciousness, began to struggle in the arms of his captors, screaming abuse.

In after years, Meriel was hard put to remember the sequence of events. Vaguely, she heard herself telling the Constable where they stayed. There were other questions put to her, but she was hardly aware of what she said, other than her accusation, which she repeated more than once.

She seemed to recall, too, that someone had

said grimly, "Well, if it be true, we'll know it soon enough."

She had a momentary fear that they had not believed her. The Constable, she thought, had looked particularly doubtful, but it did not matter. By then, thief and robbery no longer meant anything to her. All that mattered was Lord Farr's white face, his gory coat, and the blood that continued to pour from his wounded shoulder. She had heard a woman weeping and protesting as someone gently urged her from his side, Meriel had realized with a sense of shock and shame that the woman was herself. There had been a window shutter, brought from she did not know where, and placed on the ground beside him, while four stalwart young men stepped out of the crowd and, at the Constable's direction, placed his body upon it and started off in the direction of the Thistle and Shrub.

She had no clear picture in her mind as to how she reached the inn. Had she joined the great procession that followed the shutter-bearers or had the coachman driven her back? She could not remember.

Nothing really seemed clear to her until she stood in Neville Farr's chamber, holding a basin filled with reddened water, as the physician, a small, brisk man named Dr. Quigley, having cut off Lord Farr's coat and removed his shirt, cleansed the wound with whiskey and stitched it up. Having done that, he pressed a wad of cloth against the wound, tying it tightly in place.

He darted a look at her. "Did you see how I made the bandage?"

She nodded. "Yes," she answered, glad that her voice no longer shook. She added, "But will you not cup him?"

The physician frowned. "I do not hold with cupping or with leeches," he said, shortly. "He's lost a fair amount of blood already. I say . . . let him retain that which remains to him."

Meriel, whose experiences with those physicians who had attended her father, had given her a prejudice against the entire breed, was impressed. Dr. Quigley did not pontificate. He spoke with a minimum of words coupled with a calm certainty that filled her with confidence. She said, "I'd not thought of that, but it seems a highly sensible decision."

He raised his eyebrows. "Egad, I expected more opposition than that! You, my dear young lady, are also sensible. Very few members of your sex would have assisted me so calmly. Lord, in cases like these, I'm often like to have two patients on my hands."

She gave him a rueful look. "I fear I was far from calm in the beginning."

He put his hand on her shoulder. "I should not refine too much upon that, my dear. From what I understand of your experiences on the fairgrounds, you were more than entitled to a fit of the vapors. In fact, I'm told that you suffered some hurt yourself."

"It was nothing," she said, hastily. "I only had the wind knocked out of me. I am quite all right now."

He smiled. "Truly, you have my sincere admiration." Turning back to the bed, he said, "Now there's a chance that despite the stitching, the bleeding will break out afresh. If it soaks through the dressing, will you know how to change it?"

"I shall," she assured him. "I watched most closely."

"I saw that you did." He approved. "There's a chance that he might turn feverish in the night." Moving over to his bag, he brought forth a little vial and handed it to her. "This is laudanum, but I charge you, give him only a few drops of it if he's in need of calming. Now, if you'll leave the room, I'll ease him into his nightshirt."

"Of course," she assented, and hurried into the parlor, wondering uneasily what the doctor must think of her presence in Lord Farr's chambers. However, a glance at her black garments proved reassuring. Probably, he had guessed her to be a close relative. In her anguish over Lord Farr's wound, she had quite forgot to mention that she was his sister. Her thoughts were dispersed as the physician emerged.

"I will take my leave now, my dear." He smiled. "I shall return early tomorrow morning to see how he is faring."

As the doctor started toward the door, she asked the question that had been trembling on her lips throughout his ministrations. "He . . . he's not in any danger?"

Dr. Quigley shook his head. "I should think not. He seems a strong, healthy young man and, fortunately, the wound, though deep is not dangerous. No vital spot was hit. Barring infection, which I hope my application of spirits has helped to alleviate, it should heal well enough. He should be himself in less than a fortnight, I should think. Though, of course he will suffer some pain at first." He gave her a sharp look and hastened to her side. "Come, child," he slipped an arm around her. "It's no time for you to be swooning."

She said, hastily, "I am not about to swoon. It's only that I have been so worried. He looks so very pale."

He regarded her in silence for a moment. "It seems to me that you are passing pale, yourself. It might be well if I were to send a woman from the village to help nurse him."

"No, please!" she cried. "I am quite able to care for him."

He shrugged. "As you choose, but I hope you will rest at some point during the night."

"I shall," she assured him.

He looked at her doubtfully. "Very well," he said finally. "I shall bid you a good evening, then."

She nodded. "I do thank you. You've been most kind."

He patted her on the shoulder. "I was but doing my duty. Now mind, you're not to worry if he grows a bit restless. I foresee no complications." With a final reassuring pat to her shoulder, he was gone.

She hurried back into the bedchamber and, pulling a chair near to the bed, sank down upon it, staring at Neville Farr. He was propped high on his pillows, a lock of hair falling on his face, and his eyes were fast shut. Gently, she smoothed back his hair, then brought her palm down on his forehead, relieved to find it cool. As she drew her hand away, his eyes opened. He stared at her vaguely, at first, then his gaze sharpened. "Did . . . they get him?" he whispered.

She nodded. "He was remanded to the Constable."

"Good . . . good . . ." he murmured. "You . . . were very brave, Meriel."

"B-Brave," she repeated brokenly. "I . . . I would I had never seen him!"

"Come, my dear," he protested, gently. "I owe you a great deal . . . a very great deal. And you . . . you were hurt. He hit you." He frowned and raised himself upon his pillows, then winced and sank back down, stifling a groan.

"Oh, my Lord!" She was at his side in an instant. "You must not move. Your poor shoulder."

"Damn my poor shoulder. Did he hurt you?"

"No, I am quite well," she soothed. "You must lie quietly. The physician said . . ."

"Ah, yes." He nodded with a brief smile. "A competent man; I am glad he did not cup me."

She gave him a startled look. "You heard?"

"Yes, but I was not in the mood for talking."

"Nor should you talk now," she said, severely. "You must try and sleep."

"Sleep, I fear is far from me."

"The doctor's left some laudanum. I'll fetch it."

He shook his head. "I am not one for such potions," he said, firmly.

"Nor I," she agreed. "My father's physicians often prescribed them, but he'd not take them, either." She paused, saying hesitantly, "Perhaps I might be able to help you sleep."

He cocked an inquisitive eyebrow at her. "How might you do that? Would you wave a magic wand?"

She smiled. "No, my Lord, you are the magician, but my father was often restless and I used to rub his head. He said he found it very soothing. If you choose, I can do the same for you." For some reason, she felt herself flush.

His dark eyes dwelt on her face for an instant. Then he said, "I should like that, I think."

Moving to the bed, she sat on the edge of it, saying diffidently, "Should you mind if I put your head on my lap?"

Without answering, he moved carefully toward her, slipping down from his pillows until his head was resting against her.

Gently she eased his head into her lap. "Am I hurting you?" she asked him, anxiously.

"Not at all."

Putting her hands on either side of his forehead, she began to massage his temples. At first he seemed tense, but gradually, he relaxed, saying after several minutes, "You do have a magic wand. You have ten magic wands, my dear Meriel, one in each finger."

"Shhhhh," she cautioned, severely. "You must remain quiet, my Lord."

"Very well," he answered drowsily. "I do feel . . . sleepy." He closed his eyes and to her relief his breathing soon became deeper until finally he slept.

For a few moments, she sat there immobile, looking down at him. The air of authority, which characterized him when he was awake, had vanished. He looked younger and defenseless, a boy rather than a man—a boy, whom she must cosset and protect. She ran her fingers over his eyebrows and gently stroked his hair. He moved in his sleep, pushing his head against her, a little smile curling his lips.

"Love, Love," she mouthed. Reluctantly she inserted a pillow between his head and her lap, and slipping out from under it, she stepped away from the bed. She blew out the candle that stood on the nearby table and was about to return to her chair when she saw that the moon was bright upon his sleeping face. Glancing at the draperies, she went to draw them. Yet, even as she touched them, she paused, unwilling to let the darkness claim an image she wanted to commit to memory against the long years when she would see him no more.

# (8)

"Reprehensible brat!" exploded the Earl of Farringdon, glaring at his opponent. "How did you come to appropriate my rook!" Incredulously, he stared down at the shabby chess board provided earlier that afternoon by the host of the Thistle and Shrub.

Meriel, curled up at the far end of his bed, surveyed him lovingly from behind her sweeping lashes and said, virtuously, "It was not appropriated, my Lord, it was won fairly." She had been brandishing the disputed piece aloft, which now, with an elaborate flourish, she deposited beside a captured knight, a bishop, and three pawns.

He regarded her with a mixture of indignation and grudging admiration. "You are a good player," he growled. "For a female."

"If I were in a proper position to curtsey, I would." She smiled impishly.

"Blast you, you little devil. You need not gloat," he said, hotly, and then he smiled. "I expect it was your father who taught you?"

"Yes, it was his only relaxation. He had a deep prejudice against card games of any description."

"He had an apt pupil. It's not often I've lost a game—and now to be in danger of losing two in a row!" He shook his head. "I vow, I shall never live it down."

"I am sure that under other circumstances, I would not be so fortunate." She regarded him a little anxiously. "I fear that your pain is proving distracting."

He laughed. "Ah, the conqueror is disposed to be magnanimous toward her weakening foe, eh? However, my dear Meriel, I'll not take advantage of your generosity. I am distracted by nothing. I am merely out-maneuvered by a clever opponent." He stared down at the board again. "Now it remains for me to try and salvage my game—and my pride."

As he pondered his next move, Meriel, watching him, felt extraordinarily happy. Contrary to her fears, he had developed no fever during the night. Indeed, he had been tolerably comfortable and Dr. Quigley, who had, as he had promised, arrived early that morning, had found no trace of infection in the wound. She could feel doubly grateful to the little doctor, she thought, for aside from the undoubted expertise with which he had treated his patient, he had brought the news that the thief, succumbing to pressures exerted by the Constable and his men, had not only admitted robbing the castle, he had revealed the hiding place of his booty. She had another and, to her, an even greater cause for rejoicing. Lord Farr, relieved of his burden of guilt, was just as teasing and light-hearted as he had been before the regrettable incident at the castle. No, she decided, he was not quite as he had been, for at odd times during the day, she had been aware of a new warmth in his voice whenever he addressed her. There was also a softness in his glance that she had never seen before.

"Hold on," declared her spoil-sport Other Self, "he has reason to be grateful. It was you who sighted the thief and, too, there was your attendance on him."

"When he awakened, he scolded me and sent me off to bed," Meriel reminded her Other Self.

"Still, I am sure it pleased him. Do not imagine, however, that he is falling in love with you."

"I vow," Lord Farr, suddenly, said. "I stand in danger of losing my Queen as well!"

"I can but hope so, my Lord," Meriel said demurely.

His old laugh, weaker, but just as merry, rang pleasantly in her ears, "Vixen. If this carnage continues, I shall be tempted to take refuge behind my infirmity. I must have some way of maintaining my self-esteem."

"I can but think, my Lord," she said, seriously, "that it *is* your infirmity that is proving so distracting."

His eyes rested on her face. "If I am distracted, I think the cause may be traced to other origins. In fact . . ." He broke off with a little frown as they heard a sharp rap on the parlor door.

"Oh!" Meriel slipped hastily from the bed. "Perhaps it is the Constable. The landlord told me he might be up here to speak with you." Hurrying from the chamber, she was about to cross the parlor when the knock was repeated. Quickening her pace, she had reached the door when, to her amazement, she heard the sound of a key in the lock. Indignantly, she pulled open the door to find herself staring down into the discomfited contenance of the landlord, who was still holding the knob in one hand and clutching the key with the other. She was vaguely aware of other presences behind him in the shadowy hall.

"Might I ask what this intrusion signifies?" she demanded, coldly.

"Oh, M-Miss . . ." he stuttered. "I . . . feared you was not to home and the . . . er . . . this Gentleman. Uh, I mean his G-Grace, the D-Duke of Broxbridge was most desirous of seeing your b-brother."

"His Grace," Meriel said, faintly.

"A minute, if you please." A tall gentleman stepped forward, regarding Meriel out of a pair of cold, blue eyes set deep into a plump face a-top his tall, massive body. He was elegantly clad in a beautifully cut brown coat, closefitting buckskin breeches, and gleaming Hessian boots. His intricately tied cravat and stiffened shirt collar, necessarily forced his chin upward, but Meriel, noting as haughty a countenance as she had ever seen, was sure it needed no such artificial elevation. Now, in chill tones, he continued. "I have no desire to speak to the . . . brother of this young woman. I was told by the Constable that the young man who subdued the thief was residing in this Inn."

"And so he be, your Grace," the landlord said. Proudly he continued. "In this suite, as I did tell your Grace."

"Also you told me his name was Godwin, while I was under the impression that he was my cousin, the Earl of Farringdon. I cannot think how such an error was promulgated."

Meriel swallowed as she faced the Duke. She would have given much to insist that there had, indeed, been an error, but into her mind flashed an image of the Constable and herself. She knew that she must have revealed Lord Farr's true identity. With a long sigh, she said, "There has been no mistake, your Grace. Lord Farr is within." Immediately, upon her admission, she heard an outraged gasp and then, looking beyond the Duke, she saw that there were two fashionably dressed ladies standing a little farther back.

His Grace of Broxbridge raised thin eyebrows, gazing at Meriel in a way that made her long to hit him. Then, turning to the landlord, he pressed a coin into his hand. "Thank you, my good man," he said. "You may go."

"Y-Yes, your G-Grace," the landlord said. "T-Thank you, your Grace." Bowing obsequiously, he backed toward the stairs, only narrowly saving himself from falling down them in his agitation.

"I understand," pursued His Grace looking

at Meriel, "that my cousin received serious injuries in the course of his action?"

"Yes," she began, "he was hurt but . . ."

"Oh!" one of the ladies exclaimed, moving forward to stare at Meriel. "I have been wracking my brain as to where I have seen you before . . . and now I think I know."

"Beatrix," her companion protested, in outraged accents. "I beg you'll not admit to . . ."

"But I have, Mama," she insisted, taking another step forward. In doing so, she came into the light, thus affording Meriel another and most unwelcome sight—the Incomparable Miss Stansfield, resplendent, as usual, in a short and very stylish green cape, festooned with tassels and worn over a pale green walking dress, finished off by tiny, striped half-boots. Under a wide-brimmed straw hat, her lovely face was only slightly marred by the frown with which she regarded Meriel. "I do know you," she continued, in tones no less haughty than those of his Grace, the Duke of Broxbridge. "You are or have been employed in the household of Neville's uncle, Lord Lithwaite. I seem to recall that you had the capacity of Governess to young Lord Algernon. You are named after some poet or other Shakespeare, is it not?"

"I am Miss Hathaway, though no relation to the poet," Meriel repeated, automatically.

"Miss Hathaway!" Miss Stansfield said, triumphantly. "There, Mama, I knew I could not be mistaken. I never forget a name or a face." Miss Stansfield's frown deepened. "Might one know what you are doing here in the company of Lord Farr?" Her gaze narrowed. "And in widow's weeds?" A mocking little smile played about her mouth, rendering it even less attractive than Meriel had remembered. "Am I to offer my condolences?"

"Beatrix," her mother hissed. "It is not your place to inquire into these matters."

"Exactly! At least not at present," said His Grace of Broxbridge in tones that were edged with annoyance. "My dear Miss Stansfield, it would seem to me that my cousin's welfare must take precedence over other explanations." His cold eyes fell on Meriel again. "Might I know the extent of my cousin's injuries?"

"They are not serious, your Grace," Meriel replied. "The doctor is most pleased that the wound he sustained has not become infected."

"Well," Miss Stansfield observed. "That, at least, is comforting to know."

"Yes." The Duke allowed himself a slight, wintery smile. "I have often told you, my dear, that my cousin bears a charmed life." He looked at Meriel. "Might we be allowed access to my cousin's chambers?"

Conscious that she was blocking the entrance way, Meriel stepped hastily back. "Of course! Please do come in."

As the trio swept into the parlor, Meriel, more than ever aware of its shabbiness, felt wave after wave of color creep up her neck and across her face. Fixing her gaze on a point that fell in the general vicinity of rather than on her visitors, hesitantly she said, "W-Would you care to sit down?"

Instead of answering her, Miss Stansfield,

looking through her replied in icy tones, "I should like to see Lord Farr."

"Umm." The Duke cleared his throat, then addressing Miss Stansfield, he said with another touch of annoyance, "My dear lady, I think that under the circumstances, it would be better if you and your mother remained here until I have ascertained whether my cousin is able to receive you."

"Of course we must, Beatrix," the buxom Lady Stansfield snapped, giving her daughter an acerbic glance. "Lord Farr, after all, has had no preparation for your visit."

"Exactly," the Duke agreed. He bent his glacial blue gaze on Meriel, saying loftily, "If you will be so good as to show me into my cousin's bedchamber, my girl?"

Her heart was beating so rapidly that she felt she should put her hand on it to subdue its frantic pulsations, but she refrained from a gesture that might be construed as fear rather than the anger at his attitude. Drawing herself up, she said with as much dignity as she could muster, "If you will come this way, your Grace?" Swiftly, she moved across the parlor and, opening the door, stepped over the threshold. "My Lord Farr, your cousin has come to see you," she said, stiffly.

As she stepped aside to let the Duke enter, Meriel had a brief glimpse of Neville Farr's astounded face. She left the room quickly, closing the door behind her. Turning, she found herself face to face with Miss Stansfield and her mother, neither of whom had deigned to take a chair. As she exchanged glances with the two women, the full realization of her terrible predicament hit her with the force of a physical blow.

Judging from Miss Stansfield's irate glare and her mother's look of distaste, she knew they had arrived at what they believed to be the only logical explanation for Meriel's presence in Lord Farr's suite. Tears threatened to well into her eyes, but she blinked them back. It was too late to cry over the milk she had spilled in revealing Lord Farr's true identity to the Constable. In telling that particular truth, she had not only placed herself in a highly awkward position, she had prevented him from any further pursuit of the woman he loved.

Facing the Incomparable, she was appalled at the consequences of her action, for Beatrix was beautiful. She could not blame Lord Farr for adoring her. Indeed, it hardly mattered that her mouth did not measure up to her other attractions. After all, what did a mere mouth mean when you had the most speaking eyes, a Grecian nose, a swan-like neck, and lovely russet hair; not to mention an exquisite figure? Meriel, through her own folly had deprived Lord Farr of his true love. Desperately she tried to think of a way to explain her presence that would not bring more trouble down upon the head of Lord Farr. Yet, though a hundred different explanations sped rapidly through her mind, she found she must needs discard them as rapidly. Then, with a little jab of fear, she realized that there was only one that would suffice and, at the same time satisfy the Incomparable. Swallowing another lump in her throat, she said to Miss Stansfield, "I think you must know the truth."

"The truth?" Miss Stansfield repeated, coldly.

"About my presence here."

"I do not think that my daughter is interested in that particular truth." Lady Stansfield bent a baleful stare on Meriel. "I do not believe any virtuous young woman need be acquainted with such facts."

"Oh, please!" Meriel said, with a hasty glance in the direction of Lord Farr's door. "I pray that you will listen to me. It is imperative that you hear from me, for I fear that out of his innate chivalry, Lord Farr will not want me to give you the real reason for his presence in the village. I beg that you will let me tell you."

"I . . ." Lady Stansfield began, only to be quelled by a look from her daughter.

"I am prepared to hear you out, Miss Hathaway." Miss Stansfield's tone was barely civil and her manner was definitely contemptuous. Meriel felt her hackles rise, but managed to lower them. For, if she was fair, she knew she could not blame the Incomparable for her anger. She was sure it would diminish once she knew the true facts. If only she would cease to look at me as though I was the dirt under her well-shod feet, Meriel thought.

Standing very still, she began speaking, telling the story as it had occurred from the moment Lord Algernon had poured the ink onto her hair. She stressed her confusion and

157

terror, her fears for the future. She also stressed the fact that Lord Farr had promised to pay her well for her contribution to his scheme.

She was not very far into her tale before she knew that she had captured the undivided attention of her audience. She spoke of their hasty journey from village to village and much as it pained her to do so, she also mentioned Lord Farr's fear that Miss Stansfield might prefer his cousin. The Incomparable's face softened as she heard the tale. Finally, Meriel was able to give a very good account of Lord Farr's despair when his plans went awry. She conveyed the impression that much of his misery was due to the fact that he might have lost Miss Stansfield.

As she ended her tale, she pulled off her turban and veil and let her hair cascade over her shoulders.

Both women uttered little shrieks and, behind her, she heard a deeper exclamation. With a little frightened gasp, she looked around to find the Duke standing on the threshold of Lord Farr's room. She had no idea of how much he had heard until he laughed shortly and, turning on his heel, strode back into the chamber saying, "My dear Neville, better the thief than my death from shock."

She looked after him with relief. At least he was not angry. Then, to her surprise, Miss Stansfield suddenly burst into great gulping sobs. "Oh, Mama . . . Mama," she wailed.

"Good heavens, Beatrix," snapped Lady Stansfield, "do control yourself."

"Oh, Mama, I cannot. Imagine that he loved me so much he went to all that trouble just to frighten me into his arms. I cannot marry the Duke!"

"Beatrix!" Lady Stansfield said, sharply, "Keep a bridle on your tongue. He will hear you."

"I want him to hear me!" Miss Stansfield said, defiantly. "I will not marry the Duke—not when a man has demonstrated such utter, utter devotion. To think, he was nearly killed and it was all for *me*." Running lightly across the room, she stepped over Lord Farr's threshold, saying throatily, "My darling, darling Neville."

"Beatrix!" Meriel heard him exclaim.

"Yes, it's Beatrix!" she said, archly. "*Your* Beatrix, Neville."

Left alone with Lady Stansfield, Meriel found herself facing her ladyship's burning, hate-filled gaze. "Damn and blast you, little fool," she flashed. "Do you not know the harm you've wrought with your silly tongue? *You* have lost my daughter a dukedom!" With another glare, she stalked past Meriel into Lord Farr's bed chamber.

Half-blinded by tears, Meriel fled into her own chamber and snatching her hooded cloak and her reticule, she quickly crossed the deserted parlor, and pulled open the door to the hall. The last thing she heard, as she closed it behind her was the sound of Lord Farr's delighted laughter as he said, "Oh, my dear Beatrix!"

# (9)

Meriel had run and run without any direction in mind and now she sat, winded and frightened, at the edge of the road. There was a strong breeze blowing and it was raising little swirls of dust, but though she watched them, she was not thinking of them. In her ears was Lord Farr's laughter and the words she would never forget: "My dear Beatrix." She could imagine his eyes glowing as they rested on the Incomparable's lovely face. He would thrill as he heard her silly voice throbbing with pleasure at his devotion; pleasure which she probably mistook for passion rather than her own gratified conceit. She had been flattered by Meriel's explanation, which had separated Meriel from Lord Farr forever and given him back to the woman he loved.

She wondered if he would ever discover that the beautiful Beatrix did not love him, was not capable of loving anyone save her own image mirrored back to her from the eyes of her adorers. Meriel doubted he would ever be so disillusioned. His delighted laughter proved he did not know. Yet, despite its bitter consequences, she could not entirely regret the act that had brought them together. Loving him, Meriel wanted his happiness. She would have preferred him to be happy with her and, before his visitors had arrived, she had even cherished the hope that he had come to look upon her as a woman to be desired rather than as his spurious little sister. It had seemed to her that she had felt a difference in him, but his welcome to Beatrix had proved Meriel mistaken. It left her without hope.

"Oh," she moaned and felt the tears come. "I cannot cry," she said to herself, "I must go."

"Go where, go back," commanded her Other Self.

"I can't. I won't! He does not want me," she moaned, and then tensed, cocking her head. There was a sound in the air, a sound borne on the wind—music. The music of a band! "The circus," she whispered. "It is still in the village." She frowned. If they had not gone to the circus the Duke would never have learned and . . . But she could not bemoan the circumstances that had restored Lord Farr's spirits and, at the same time, resulted in the capture and confession of the thief.

Unwillingly, she remembered the first time they had gone there—to see the magician and the Gypsy, Madame Astra. Thinking about her, she remembered her words again. They had confused and frightened her, but they had been accurate. There had been pain and bloodshed. She had talked of tears and a parting, and of two journeys—a longer one and a shorter one. Were these the journeys that awaited her now, and which one should she take? Should she try to go to Bath or . . . She ran her hands through her hair! What would the woman at Bath think if she were suddenly to arrive there babbling of Lord Farr, and with blue hair?"

"My hair, my hair," she moaned out loud. "Oh, I do feel so confused. Maybe Madame Astra could advise me. I need advice from someone, and she did sound wise and kind."

It was kindness that decided her. Intimidating as the Gypsy had been, she had also generated a warmth that Meriel, so soon to be thrust into a world of strangers, felt she needed.

"Also you need to know if you will ever see Lord Farr again," remarked her Other Self. "You could see him easily enough, were you to return to the inn. Return! Return! Return!" It urged, begged, commanded.

"No, I can't! I must go away from Lord Farr. I must not think of seeing him again, ever!" Those thoughts, turned into a sort of litany, pounded in her head as she walked, her feet bearing her toward the sound of the music. Soon she was at the entrance to the fairgrounds, only vaguely aware that she was weary from her long tramp over the hard roads, weary and unexpectedly warm.

As usual, there were crowds milling around and as she came in, she realized that she had entered that section of the fairgrounds given over to the Oddities. She drew a long tremulous breath and blinked moisture from her eyes. It was here that she and Lord Farr had come only yesterday. She had an impulse to run out and find another entrance, but looking back she found that more people had poured in behind her and the idea of pushing through them daunted her. Resignedly, she went on ahead, trying not to look at the banners and the posters, but if she could manage that, she could not shut out the noise of the place. It was even worse than she remembered—the sounds confused her. Her head began to ache. She felt feverish, but perhaps that was due to her hood. It was too warm to wear a hood. Unthinkingly, she thrust it back and tried to push on, but it was so difficult to worm her way through the crowds. It would be easier to go around to the backs of the tents. She stepped off the path and started toward one of them, only to be halted by a crowd of people just coming out of one of the sideshows.

" 'Ere," somebody said in amazement. "Wot's this?"

She looked up at a huge man standing directly in front of her staring down at her. "Please let me pass," she said, coldly.

He did not move. Instead, he took a handful of her hair and held it up. "By all that's 'oly, she's got blue 'air."

Meriel paled. She had forgotten about her hair! She tried to pull away, but to no avail. The man retaining his hold. She reached for her hood, but somebody else was touching her hair and asking in a thick ugly voice, "Did it grow that way?"

Before she knew it, she was surrounded by people, who stared and poked and pulled at her, "Let me go," she cried. "Let me alone!"

They remained where they were, marveling, speculating, staring, and examining. She pushed at them in vain. Then, suddenly, a short swarthy man barreled his way through the gathering crowd. "'Ere," he began, glaring about him belligerently, "Wot d'ye mean blockin' my entrance?" Then his eyes fell on Meriel and they widened. "Oo're you?" he demanded.

Meriel, meeting a stare that was at once curious and fierce, faltered. "I was looking for Madame Astra."

"Ye've got blue 'air," he rasped, reaching up a short pudgy hand to scratch his own thick curling black hair. "Where'd you get blue 'air?"

"Maybe she's a mermaid," remarked someone. "I've 'eard as mermaids've got green 'air."

"An fish tails. She ain't got a fish tail," a woman jeered.

Meriel stared at the man who had interrogated her. He was brightly dressed in a red vest and dark green breeches thrust into cracked brown boots. There was an air of authority about him, which made her believe that he was connected with the circus. "Please, I must see Madame Astra. Will you direct me to her tent?"

He gave her a long frowning look. "Madame Astra, is it? I expect I could."

"Oh, would you? I should like to see her and I must needs leave town soon."

He hesitated, still staring at her hair. "All right, come this way." He jerked a thumb over his shoulder and turned in the direction of the tents. Then, glancing at the people around him, he added, " 'Awri, awri, move along. Let us through."

Somewhat to Meriel's surprise, they made way for him. Then, stealing a side glance at him, she was not so surprised. Though he was not tall, he had a broad chest and great muscular arms. In addition to a broken nose, he had scars on his face, which suggested he might have been a pugilist. She said, gratefully, "You are kind. I do thank you for rescuing me."

He shrugged. "Ye don't need to thank me. But your 'air. 'Ow'd you come by it?"

"It's dyed," she said. "It was an accident. Someone poured ink on my head, and then there was a p-plan . . ." She broke off, blinking away threatening tears. "I really don't want to talk about it. If you could show me where I might find Madame Astra?"

"I will. Come this way."

They had reached the backs of the tents and she found herself in a small clearing. On the other side of it, there were several caravans. He led her past these, stopping at one that was located some distance away. She looked at it in some surprise. It bore traces of having once been painted red, but exposure to the elements together with the passing of time had worn off the paint. Only patches of it remained; the rest was a dull, grayish brown. Dingy curtains hung in the windows facing her and there was a heap of foul-smelling trash near the steps that led to its door. She looked at it with distaste. "Is this where she lives?" she inquired, amazed.

"No, but I wanted my wife to see your 'air." He flashed her a smile, which was evidently meant to be engaging, but which emerged more as a snarl, exposing broken, yellowed teeth.

"Oh!" Meriel wanted to protest, but since he had been kind enough to get her away from her tormentors, she said nothing.

Stepping closer to the steps of his caravan, the man bellowed, "Liddy, come 'ere."

"Wot d'yer want?" yelled a voice from within.

"Come 'ere," he repeated. "I got somethin' for ye to see."

"Aw'right," she returned, in a dry, rasping tone. In another moment, a thin, narrow-eyed woman, clad in a drab, faded gown, jerked open the door of the caravan, "Wot?" she demanded, staring at Meriel suspiciously. "Oo's she?"

The man jerked Meriel's hood back. "Look at 'er 'air."

Meriel uttered a cry of indignation, "Please!" she began.

"Oh, c'mon," he said with another of his fearsome smiles,

"Let Liddy see. It won't 'urt, will h'it."

"N-No," Meriel said, reluctantly, and then shrank away as the woman grabbed a length of her hair.

"Dyed," she rasped.

"Yes, but it 'as possibilities," he said. "Out there they was about 'er like flies."

"P-Possibilities?" Meriel stuttered. "I don't understand. Please, you said you'd direct me to Madame Astra. Couldn't we be on our way?"

He gave her a long measuring look. "Wot's yer 'urry?" he demanded. "You got your sweetie waitin' for yer?"

She drew herself up. "I do not have anyone, but I am leaving town and . . ."

"Where're you goin'?" demanded the woman.

"London," Meriel said. "Now, if you will excuse me . . ."

"London, is it?" growled the man. "Wot will ye do in London?"

"I will find work," Meriel told him, coldly, speaking with considerably more confidence than she felt.

"Work?" He stared at her. " 'Ow'd you like to work wi' us."

"With you?" she repeated.

"My name's Matthew Swain 'n' this 'ere's my wife. I got me an exhibit: a pin-'eaded boy 'n' a two-'eaded calf 'n' a six-legged lamb. I could use you. They liked you, the crowds. Your 'air!"

She looked at him incredulously, "You mean as an Oddity?"

"Yes," the woman said. "We'd give you a gown 'n' put you in the center of the tent. We'd pay you good 'n' you could travel wi' us."

*I could be Bertha, the Blue-headed Woman.* The words went through her head. In

167

spite of the misery they conjured up, she still felt an insane desire to giggle. She stifled it. "Oh, no, I couldn't really."

"Why not?" demanded Mrs. Swain. "It ain't 'ard work. All you do is sit."

"I am sure it is very easy," Meriel replied. "But my hair is dyed. I really could not qualify as an Oddity."

"Wot difference does that make," Mr. Swain rasped. "Them wot come 'ere likes to be bamboozled'n' 'alf'd believe yer 'air grew like that. I could see they liked you. You'd be a big draw. Why'n't you give it a try 'n' see."

"No!" Meriel was beginning to find his insistence wearing. "I couldn't possibly." She started to turn away. "I would not want you to think I am not grateful for your offer, but please . . . If you will show me the way to Madame Astra?"

Mrs. Swain shrugged, "Show 'er, Matt. Show 'er 'ow."

"Thank you and . . ." Meriel turned, then froze—a fist was coming at her and, before she could move, it had hit her chin. She felt terror, there was pain and brightness behind her eyes, then oblivion.

She was thirsty, dreadfully thirsty, and her stomach pained her terribly. She craved food, but she had had nothing to eat for three days and very little water to drink. Tears of weakness forced themselves between her closed lids and rolled down her cheeks. She could not wipe them away. Her hands were bound behind her back; her feet were bound, too. The ropes bit into her flesh and the gag over her mouth was stifling, but she no longer moaned or struggled. She had in the beginning. Once she had recovered consciousness to find her clothes gone and her body covered only with a thin, dirty shift. She was lying bound on the caravan floor. She had wept, pleaded, and even screamed until she was cuffed into silence by Mrs. Swain.

"We give ye yer chance, girl 'n' ye wouldn't take it. But we want ye 'n' ye're comin' wi' us," she had said, roughly.

"I won't! I won't!" Meriel had cried between her bruised lips.

"Ye'll come round," Mrs. Swain said, grimly. "One way or t'other ye'll come round." She had moved back to call, "Swain."

He had come, then, to glare down at her out of his fierce eyes. "Ye'll pull 'em in, girl, better'n the sheep or the pin-'ead. I seen 'ow they looked at you outside." He had grinned. "We got an idea as 'ow you're goin' to be a mermaid wi' blue 'air. That's wot."

"You . . . you're mad." She had wept. "I s-shan't."

"Tell me that in a week," he had responded, still grinning.

A week had not gone by yet, but she was terribly hungry, so terribly hungry and so thirsty. A moan she could not stifle burst from her and she moved restlessly. The floor suddenly shook. She knew what that meant. One of the Swains was coming. Rolling her eyes up, she saw Mrs. Swain standing over her. The woman knelt down and loosened the gag. "You hungry?" she demanded.

Meriel wanted to shake her head, but she

**169**

could not keep herself from whispering, "Y-yes."

"You goin' to be good?"

Again, Meriel longed to defy her, but she smelled food, fresh-baked bread and cheese. Then, she saw that Mrs. Swain was holding a wooden trencher. She eyed it avidly. "Yes," she said.

"You promise?"

"Yes," Meriel half-sobbed, staring at the bowl.

"Swear it. Swear it on yer mother's 'ead."

"On my mother's . . . head." She wept, hating her weakness.

Mrs. Swain undid the ropes that bound her wrists and slid the bowl along the floor. "All right, eat, but not too fast, mind."

Meriel did not hear her. Propping herself up on her elbow, she used her other hand to break off a great hunk of cheese. She shoved it into her mouth and swallowed hastily; Then she bit off pieces of the bread, and barely chewing it, swallowing again. Convulsively, she repeated the process until she gagged and choked.

"I tol' ye to go easy," Mrs. Swain growled. Hastily she handed her a mug of water. Meriel swallowed it but she continued to gag and choke until her stomach rejected the food and she lay retching weakly, wishing she would die.

She was hardly aware of Mrs. Swain wiping her face. "Shouldn't 've et it so fast," she said. "Gotta go slow when you ain't 'ad nothin' for a bit."

She nodded. She was too tired to accuse

them of starving her, too tired to say a single word. Later, she did not know how much later, Mrs. Swain gave her hot tea to drink. After that, Meriel slept.

The caravan was moving. The Swains were quarreling. They were always quarreling, his voice, loud, growing louder, as if he would cow his wife through mere volume rather than argument, which was ineffective because he had an insufficient supply of words to illustrate his thoughts. His words were spaced out into sentences through the addition of meaningless oaths.

Mrs. Swain never ran out of words. Hers was a dry, yellowed voice, sounding much like its aging owner looked. It grated on the ears, wore down the ears the way endless water drops wear holes in stones.

Beneath their harsh voices there were other sounds, the rattling of the harnesses on the team of horses, the snorting and whinnying of the tired beasts as they plodded onward, dragging the heavy caravan behind them. It had its own sound as it swayed from side to side —a wrenching of old wood, a scraping of metal. Meriel, huddled on a thin straw pallet, had a sound, too, the metal clink of the chain that bound her to the stake Mr. Swain had pounded into the floor after she became their property. Lying sleepless on her pallet, she wondered where they were going.

It was not a very active wondering because the destination no longer mattered. All places were the same, whether they were called Escrick or Torworth or Bawtry. There were the fairgounds, the crowds of the tent and, now, there was the discomfort of sitting in the tail. Yet, she was past complaining. She would not risk the punishment that had followed her one attempt to communicate with the people who crowded the tent after she had been put on display. She had dared to cry out to them, to beg and plead for help, only to receive blank glances and then laughter as Mrs. Swain explained that she was homesick for the grotto wherein the sharks had nursed her. In the first two weeks, she was known as the "Shark Maiden" because they had not finished building the tail.

Meriel had wondered why those who crowded into the tent were so willing to believe Mr. Swain's lies. She knew now that they wanted to believe him. They were farmhands and dairymaids in a mood to make merry on their one day off. They loved to be shocked by the India-Rubber Man, the Two-Headed Calf, the Python Man, and by the Shark Maiden with the blue hair, who was only another oddity, as much a freak as the Legless Wonder or the horrifying Frog Woman, whose goggling eyes and wide mouth made even strong men faint.

She shivered in retrospect as she remembered the results of her bid for freedom. Mrs. Swain had pinched her, squeezing her tender flesh until she was on fire with pain, until she forgot all pride and lay sobbing for mercy, until she promised never, never to call out again or to do anything to incur their displeasure—and she had not.

For the last month she had been totally docile, even when they had built the tall tank, which shut most of the air away from her and made her feel dreadfully hot. But the tail was worse. Thinking about it, she winced. It had been expensive to mold. It had been fashioned from plaster of Paris, cunningly painted, and decorated to resemble a long shining fishtail. She was thrust into it for five shows, and it was terribly uncomfortable. It pressed her feet together until they ached intolerably. Once she was in it, she could tell from the reactions of the crowd that she looked impressive—with her face whitened, her eyes elongated with liner, and her long blue hair flowing over her bare shoulders. She was a very popular exhibit. No one knew how much she suffered, and if they had known, they would not have cared. Oddities were born without feelings.

There was silence, now, the Swains were no longer quarreling. They lay across from her in their separate cots: he snoring and she sleeping quietly and closer to Meriel because of the time the woman had caught him fondling her. Meriel shrank away from that particular memory, which was, perhaps, the most frightening one of all. It was the most agonizing because it brought to mind Lord Farr and Beatrix. That was not true, it could not bring him to mind, because he was never wholly out of her mind. When tears stole into her eyes; she blinked them away, because if she were not careful, she might sob aloud and be punished. Defensively, she closed her eyes and, finally, she slept.

173

The lights in the tent were dim and the great glass tank in which the mermaid was kept had the appearance of a sea grotto. There were rocks around her and a luridly painted backdrop of fancifully colored seaweed behind her. There were real shells scattered about and the whole so cunningly arranged that no one out front knew that the blue-haired girl sitting on the rock was chained to the stake that forced her to remain upright. She was not always on view. There were other exhibits in the tent, a two-headed calf that sometimes mooed in a loud and frightening way, the sound issuing from its twin throats. There was also a six-legged lamb, but the poor creature had a dreadful time keeping upright and was often falling over and being picked up, roughly, by its keeper, Mr. Swain. Swain also gave the signal to the lad who raised and lowered the curtain on the mermaid. She was seen last and the curtain stayed up for about ten minutes.

The curtain had been raised and lowered twice and was now slowly rising again. Meriel looked apathetically at it, not really seeing it, just as she would not really see the faces of those who were waiting to stare at her. She had a headache. Her hair had been dyed blue again that morning and the stuff they had used hurt her scalp. The first time they had put it on, she had protested violently, but a box on her ear had silenced her. Since then, it had been applied on two more occasions, roughly rubbed in by Mrs. Swain, who protested that the task was a great nuisance since it took so long to get the blue off her fingers. The curtain was up. Meriel caught Swain's angry brown eyes upon her and hastily she smiled. It was the expression she must maintain for ten minutes. It was difficult to smile steadily for ten minutes, but when the curtains rolled down again, she would be given some lemonade. She needed the liquid. Her throat was dry. She wished that the ten minutes would come to an end soon.

She tensed, suddenly, as two men came very near the tank. Mr. Swain would not like that. He had signs posted about, warning people off, suggesting that anyone approaching too closely would frighten the wild creature within. Usually this warning was heeded, for he strolled about the tent and his muscular body gave the impression of great strength, just as his fierce dark eyes hinted at an ungovernable temper. There had been times when he had thrown importunate customers out of the tent. She wondered if the two men were in danger. It hardly mattered, but if there was an altercation, it might be some minutes before he lowered the curtain and she would have to wait longer for the lemonade. She swallowed, but her tongue stuck to the roof of her mouth and felt fuzzy.

Her heart sank. They were coming closer, and behind them, she saw Mr. Swain, his eyes fairly shooting out sparks of anger. She wondered at their temerity and, for the first time, she realized that they were foreigners—East Indians. They both wore white turbans and one of them was very dark. He was tall, too, and possibly seemed taller because he was bone thin. He wore a beard and moustache and was clad in the dress of his native land. The man with him was not quite as dark. He was shorter and there was something familiar about him. Then, suddenly she recognized him and with a little thrill of joy, knew him to be the Great Khan. Moved by an impulse she did not know she still possessed, she leaned forward eagerly, trying to catch his eye, actually daring to wave at him. At that moment, Mr. Swain was upon them, and she caught his furious eyes staring at her. She shrank back, trembling.

The Great Khan, however, was unperturbed as was the Indian with him. Both went docilely enough from the tent while Meriel sank back against her stake, wondering why she had been so foolish as to try and signal him, for out of the depths of her memory, she recalled that he had never seen her face. She had been veiled, a young widow with her solicitous brother. Despairingly she continued to smile, but her head ached and her throat was dry, so very dry. She knew there would be no lemonade to relieve it.

The crowds continued to pour into the tent until very late. It was close to midnight when the Swains unlocked her chains and lifted her from the tail. Because of the long hours she had spent cramped inside of it, she could not walk, and Mr. Swain carried her back to the caravan.

She hung limply in his great arms, hardly feeling the surreptitious movements of his hands against her body until Mrs. Swain, who strode at his side, suddenly dealt him a stunning blow on the side of the head, growling, "Mind wot ye're about."

Finally, Meriel was back on her pallet, clad in her tattered, dirty shift. Her cramped legs pained her, but she hardly noticed that discomfort, for Mrs. Swain was standing over her and she knew there was a worse agony in store for her. Trembling, she tried to steel herself against it. Under her breath, she whispered, "I will not cry. No matter what she does, I will be brave this time. I will, I will." Then, Mrs. Swain was kneeling beside her, her hands curved like talons. Meriel with a piteous little moan shrank as far away from her as she could.

The thin, hard fingers were all over her, squeezing her tender flesh until she could contain herself no longer, and screamed, "Please don't h-hurt me! Don't . . . Don't . . . don't . . . please . . . please . . ." But the hurt continued, longer than usual, much longer, and when it stopped she lay limp, sobbing hysterically until a slap across her face finally silence her.

"You little fool," the woman hissed, "tryin' to get the eye of one o' us. He won't have no use for ye . . . none've'm will. I tell ye, it'll go worse wi' ye next time. It's time ye got that through yer thick 'ead. There's things'll 'urt worse'n pinches. Things as'll make ye wish ye was never born. So ye remember that." Grabbing a length of Meriel's blue hair, she wrenched her face off the pillow where she had buried it and glared into her eyes. "Ye remember that."

"Yes," Meriel quavered and then, because she could not help herself, she mumbled, "Water . . . please water."

"Not tonight." Mrs. Swain smiled. "Ye'll go dry tonight, my girl: Maybe it'll help ye remember."

She said nothing more. There was no reason to say anything. To beg for water would only please her tormentor and she would gain nothing by it. She lay quietly, waiting for all the pains to cease, and she thought about the Great Khan, who had inadvertently caused her present woe.

The Indian must have been his assistant. She remembered that he had once offered that position to Lord Farr. She bit down a sob, remembering how she had run from him that fatal afternoon—run to the circus, to the Gypsy, to learn about her future. Well, she had not found the Gypsy, but she had found her future. Then, from deep in her mind, she heard Madame Astra's voice: *"I see tears and parting. I see losing and winning. I see good and I see evil—and I see a short journey and a longer one. I see a weary wait and a cold fire, but its flames will warm you. . . . I am to remind you that there is the time of blossoming."*

Strange words that she had forgotten and now remembered. There had been tears and a parting, there had been loss, there had been evil, and there had been a long journey and a weary wait. All that had come to pass—all the evil. Might she hope that she might experience the good as well? What had the Gypsy meant by "a cold fire" with warm flames and the time of blossoming?

She sighed. It was futile to hope. She would never escape the Swains, unless it was by death. It occurred to her that she did not expect to live very long. Her body was weakening; she knew that. She had fainted twice the previous week. She felt ill a good deal of the time. She had lost her appetite, for who could enjoy the messes served by Mrs. Swain. Another few months of this life and she might very well succumb. It was not a thought that frightened her. It . . . Suddenly she tensed. She'd heard a sound, footsteps outside; that surprised her. She rarely heard footsteps near the Swain's caravan. It stood by itself, a good distance from any of the others.

There was a knock on the door. That was even more surprising! As long as she had been with the couple, she had never known anyone to knock on their door. It was a loud knock, but both of them were fast asleep and neither stirred. The knock was repeated and this time it was very loud.

"Oo's there?" Mr. Swain growled, sleepily.

"Please to answer, Sahib," she heard a man say. He had a thick foreign accent.

"Wot d'ye want?" Mr. Swain demanded.

"Please, I must warn you," the man urged.

"Warn me?"

"Garn'see wot 'e wants," Mrs. Swain ordered.

"Damn 'n' blast the bugger!" Mr. Swain rose and stumbled across the floor to jerk open the door. "Well?"

"I am sorry to trouble you, Sahib," the man said, very deferentially. "But it is that I have lost my snake and my Master, the Great Khan, insists that I tell you."

"Your snake!" exclaimed Mr. Swain. "An'·

179

wot am I supposed to do about it at this hour? 'Elp ye find h'it?"

"But no, Sahib, it is to warn you that I have come. I am warning all those who are on the lot . . . especially those who, as you, are camped where the grass grows high. Tomorrow when you descend, you must look where you step."

"Ye be with the magician?" Mr. Swain asked.

"He is my master, Sahib. This evening I came with him to see your exhibit, the mermaid. Ah, she is very beautiful."

There was a sudden movement near Meriel and Mrs. Swain's hand clamped tightly down on her mouth.

Meriel did not struggle. It was no use to struggle. She had not even wanted to cry out. She had only been listening.

In the front of the caravan, the Great Khan's assistant said, "Well, I must warn others about my snake. Did I explain that she is a cobra?"

"A cobra!" Mr. Swain echoed, furiously. "Why'n Hell didn't ye keep h'it fast?"

"But, Sahib, I thought that I had," the man said, politely. "I do not know how she came to escape. I pray, I will soon find her. Meanwhile, I beg you be careful of the high grass and I bid you good night."

"Damned heathen bugger!" snarled Mr. Swain, slamming the door behind his unwelcome guest. "Wot's 'e doin' wi' a poisonous snake, anyway?"

Meriel puzzled over that; puzzled over the fact that she had seen the man earlier in the tent. Was it true about the snake or was there a chance that he had been looking for *her?* Had he seen something in her face that might have aroused his sympathy. She bit back a sigh. She was being tantalized by hope, but she had already learned that it was useless to hope. Hope was a disease. Closing her eyes, she prayed for the brief oblivion of sleep, but now she smelled something strange, something acrid. She covered her nose, still it persisted and she began to cough. The Swains were also coughing. There was more than an odor in the caravan; there was smoke, thick, yellow smoke!

"God, we're on fire!" Mr. Swain yelled and was echoed by his wife, who scrambled to her feet. Coughing and sputtering they stumbled to the door. She heard it open. She also thought she heard a cry, but she could not be sure. Then, she was frightened, terribly frightened for she would not be able to escape the flames. Chained as she was, she would burn to death once they reached her straw pallet. She screamed and screamed out of her dry, hoarse throat. Then someone was beside her.

"Come, come," a voice urged, a voice she remembered but could not, in her panic, place.

"I cannot," she sobbed. "I am chained."

*"Chained!"* the word was repeated in a voice so distorted by fury as to sound scarcely human. "Where is this chain?" demanded her rescuer. She shook her wrist. He grasped it and pulled, but the smoke was heavy and it was growing heavier. She coughed and choked. In a moment, she would suffocate. Despair, worse than any she had known during

all her weeks of captivity, claimed her, for, at the moment when she might have been rescued, hope had played its cruelest trick on her and she knew that she was about to die. With a little moan, she fell forward.

# (10)

Meriel awakened on softness and in darkness. The softness was beneath her and the darkness all around her. She moved and found herself touching smoothness, soft smoothness. Linen? It *was* linen, lovely linen, scented with lavender—linen sheets. She did not understand how she came to be lying between linen sheets. She did not need to understand. She turned over carefully so as not to pull on her chained wrist, but her wrist was no longer chained. She could move it freely, could move both arms freely! She could take any position she chose!

It was very puzzling, especially since she had expected to die. Of course, there was the possibility that she had died and was now in heaven. Yet, the Vicar, who had preached in the church at Chalfont St. Giles had never mentioned anything about lavender-scented linen sheets in heaven. His descriptions had run to gates of pearl and golden streets. She smiled at the memory and was surprised. She could not remember having wanted to smile of her own accord for a long time, but now, touching the sheets, she smiled and then, her eyelids felt weighted, and she closed them again and slept.

Afternoon sun filled the chamber. Meriel, opening drowsy eyes, looked about her in amazement. Instead of the drab sides of the caravan with its dirty windows and stained curtains; instead of the narrow length of flooring cluttered with battered pots and pans, chipped dishes, old clothing, and the two cots belonging to the Swains, she was looking at green paneled walls hung with steel engravings of eighteenth-century beauties, at a deep-pile gold carpet, at a wide fireplace under a mantelshelf on which stood a small Dresden clock ornamented with china flowers and topped by a cup-bearing cupid. Directly above her was a huge square of gathered golden silk, which, she realized in another moment, was part of the canopy on an immense four-poster bed. She pulled herself up against soft down-filled pillows. There was a stirring and the sound of a chair being pushed back.

Turning around, she tensed, for there was a man rising to his feet. He stepped quickly to the side of the bed, looking down at her out of dark eyes sunk in deep hollows. Then, amazingly, he knelt and taking one of her hands, he pressed it to his lips, kissing it passionately. "Oh, my love, my dearest, dearest love," he murmured brokenly. "I thought . . . I thought I should never see you again."

She stared at him incredulously, shocked by the sight of his hollowed eyes and pale cheeks and by a body grown so thin that his clothes hung on him. She was confused, not only by his changed appearance but by his presence. "I must be feverish," she whispered. "Else, I'd not see . . .

"It's no fever, love." Now his hand was on her hair brushing it back gently. He leaned forward to kiss her and she saw that his cheeks were wet with tears. Then, he drew back hastily. "No, I must wait. Sleep, my own beloved, sleep."

"But, if I am not feverish, then I must be sleeping, for dreams come only when one sleeps and I must be dreaming that I see you, my Lord Farr." With a shuddering intake of breath, she said, "I have tried so hard not to dream of you. For always there has been the awakening. It is easier to dream of nothing." Fretfully, she moved against her pillows, "Oh, please, go away, for if you do not, I shall not want to awaken and I must."

"No, I shan't go yet, not until you know that you are here with me and safe. Not until you know that sleeping or waking, I will never let you out of my sight again." Rising, he sat on the edge of the bed and reaching for her, he gathered her body into his arms. "I am with you, my Meriel," he said and beneath her ear, she heard the steady beat of his heart. His arms were tight about her, he rested his chin lightly on the top of her head. "You see how neatly your body folds into mine?" he asked, tenderly.

She could no longer doubt the evidence of all her senses. "You are here," she discovered. "So thin . . . so pale." In alarm, she cried, "You have been ill."

"Not ill," he corrected, "only nearly driven distracted by fear. Fear of what might have happened to you, my Meriel, my love." His voice broke, and she felt his lips on her hair and then against her cheek.

"But, Miss Stansfield," she breathed.

His arms tightened. "There is no Miss Stansfield," he said, sharply. Then, his voice softened. "There is but one woman in my life and her name is Meriel. Now, my dearest, dearest love, I pray you get well quickly, for I have been far too long without you."

In the beginning, Dr. Quigley had been as insubstantial an image as her visions of Lord Farr, worn to a mere shadow of himself, and alternately caressing her and cursing the Swains. However, by what one of the soft-voiced maids, who came and went in her chamber, told her was the fifth day since she had been brought back to Broxbridge Village and thence to the castle, she was nearly herself again, and if the terrible ordeal of the past six weeks was not yet entirely blotted from her mind, at least, it was much diminished. She no longer awakened expecting to hear the quarreling voices of the Swains or to feel the jouncing of the caravan. A certain stiffness remained in her legs, but that was going away through the massage, the physician had recommended. She was eating more. She had been able to eat very little in the beginning, she had been starved too long.

Dr. Quigley said it was the nourishment she had received that had helped revive her spirits and speed her recovery but she, listening to him, and nodding dutifully, knew that the real "cure" was standing at her side, still looking anxious, although the dark circles around his own eyes were finally vanishing and his wasted body filling out. Meriel wished that Dr. Quigley might go away and leave her with Lord Farr, but the physician, usually so sparing of words, was waxing eloquent. However, as she listened impatiently, she was pleased to hear him say, "I see no reason why she cannot be taken into the garden. It is a fine day, but mind you, my Lord, she is not to remain there too long—an hour at the most."

"Your orders will be strictly obeyed," Lord Farr said, seriously, his eyes straying to Meriel, as they always did, almost as if he were reassuring himself as to her presence.

"Then, I bid you both a good morning," the physician said.

Lord Farr insisted on carrying her down into the gardens. She protested, "Your shoulder!"

He winced and there was a look of pain in his eyes as he answered, "But it has been healed for weeks, my dearest."

The gardens of Broxbridge Hall were extensive. There were great patterned plots and there was a vista centered by an immense fountain. The spot to which Lord Farr brought Meriel was, perhaps, the most beautiful of all.

Surrounded by tall, clipped hedges, it consisted of a marble platform on which stood gigantic pink-and-white alabaster urns filled with flowering plants and vines. Running the length of the platform was an oblong pool on which floated purple water-lilies, while among them a school of fat red carp swam languidly.

There were two wide wicker chairs and a table set on the platform. After he had gently deposited Meriel in one of the chairs, Lord Farr proceded to put a light wool coverlet over her.

"No." She smiled. "I am quite warm in this." She ran her hand over her peignoir, looking at it admiringly. It was the loveliest one she had ever seen—made of white silk, edged with lace, and embroidered with yellow butterflies hovering over pale blue flowers. Beneath it, she wore a lawn nightdress, also edged with lace. The garments, she had been told, belonged to the Duke's late mother. She said, "It was kind of his Grace to let me wear these lovely garments. I should like to thank him."

"You must wait." Lord Farr smiled. "Rex has gone off to Italy."

"On a honeymoon?" Meriel could not help asking.

"No, my love." A gleam of mischief shone briefly in Lord Farr's eyes. "His agent has told him of a Giambologna bronze in Florence, which he might be able to buy. Rex does not have any matrimonial plans at present. Now, are you sure you will be warm enough?"

"Quite sure," she told him.

"Very well," he said. Pulling the other chair close, he sat down and took her hand.

She looked at him adoringly. It was wonderful, she thought, to be near him and to hear his loving words, but she was confused by them, confused, too, by all that had happened. For along with her increasing strength had come curiosity. Now, as the silence deepened between them, she could bear it no longer. "You must tell me how you came to find me," she begged. "Please, tell me everything."

He gave her a look so tender, so loving that her heart turned over, but he said, "The doctor has told me that I must not tire you."

"Oh, please," she protested. "I shall be so much more tired if I do not know."

He hesitated, "But . . ."

"Please," she pressed his hand.

His grasp tightened. "Very well, since he has also told me I must humor the patient."

As he had done once eons before, it seemed to her now, he began to recount all that had happened, and he told it vividly enough to make her see it through his eyes. He started with a description of his emotions on seeing his cousin stride into his bedroom at the Thistle and Shrub, asking him bluntly, how he had happened to know the identity of the thief who had robbed the castle. It had been embarrassing and painful for him to confess the truth, but amazingly enough, Rex had been exceptionally forbearing.

"Had he not retrieved the stolen goods, I doubt he would have been quite so conciliating," Lord Farr had commented dryly to Meriel. "But be that as it may, he was grateful. Then he went to fetch Miss Stansfield and her mother, but before he reached her, she came running in full of protestations of love; so patently false that I could not control my laughter."

"You laughed at her?" Meriel whispered.

He nodded. "It was most ungentlemanly of me, but I was in too weakened a condition to control myself. Furthermore, I took great satisfaction in telling her, 'My dear Beatrix, I am already affianced.' His eyes darkened. "I . . . I called you, but you did not come." His voice trembled. "Oh, Meriel, why did you run away?"

"I thought you would want me to go. I did not want to be a burden to you. I knew that Miss Stansfield . . ."

"Damn Miss Stansfield," he said, explosively. "How could you think that I would wish you to go? Could you not see . . . did you not know how very much I had come to love you?"

"You did not say so."

"Oh, God!" he burst out. "I would have told you that very afternoon. I was primed to tell you when my cursed cousin and his retinue arrived. And for that you have endured so much, and I might never have found you."

"But you did find me," she reminded him, gently. "Yet, I cannot think how. How could you have known where to seek me?"

"I did not know," he groaned. "I knew nothing at first. When they told me you had gone, I thought you might have been intimidated by the Duke. I could hardly wait for them to leave. I thought you would come back immediately, but you did not. I called the landlord, but he had not seen you go. No one had.

I waited long into the night, thinking you would return, but you did not. I was beside myself with fear. At dawn, I rose from my bed intending to ride after you."

"Oh, how could you think of such a thing," she gasped. "Your shoulder."

"Yes," he said, bitterly. "My damn shoulder. My wound opened and I was bedded for a fortnight."

"Oh, Neville," she wept. "How could you have been so rash?"

"How could I not, loving you as I did and knowing you were almost penniless. Knowing, too, that you were such an innocent and without me to protect you . . . I had such fears, such terrible fears! I saw you ravished or dead." He broke off, then continued, chokingly, "Even now it is hard to talk of that time. Each hour seemed to last forever. I had so used to having you at my side, and not to have you there . . ." He paused again and bringing her hand to his lips, he kissed it. "But you are here. I have found you and, by God, I shall never let you go again."

"Oh, my dearest love," she murmured. "I shall never want to leave you." Then, after a moment's silence, she asked, "But you've not yet told me how you were able to find me."

"It was after I'd been to my uncle's house in London, though why I should have dreamed you would go there, I do not know. I was not thinking clearly. I knew only that since I had not found you in Chalfont St. Giles or at Bath with Miss Chance, I must search for you *somewhere*. Then, as I came forth from Lithwaite

191

Mansion, I heard the music of a military band in Hyde Park and, suddenly, I was reminded of the circus and in my head, I heard you say, 'I could be Bertha, the Blue-Headed Woman.'"

He gave her a stricken look. "You had laughed and I, wrapped in my own anger and frustration, had scolded you for reminding me of my foolishness. Afterward, we'd happened upon the thief and you'd been so brave— but I digress, I fear. Listening to the sound of that band, I remembered, too, that the circus had been in the village. I wondered if you might not have joined it. I could hardly believe you'd have done anything so dangerous, so foolhardy, but it was an outside chance and I decided to act upon it. By then, I should have done anything, anything." His voice thickened and he was silent for a moment. Then, staring at her almost accusingly, he said, "What possessed you to go to the circus —and how did the Swains get you?"

"I wanted to see the the Gypsy," she faltered. "I was wearing my hood. It was a warm day so I threw it back, and all the people crowded about me and stared. I couldn't get past them until Mr. Swain helped me. He said he'd direct me to Madame Astra, and then he and his wife, they made me go with them." Her eyes filled with tears, "I cannot talk about it. Not yet, not yet." She buried her face in her hands.

"Oh, my love, I shouldn't have asked you." He put his arms around her. "I must take you back to your chamber and let you rest. Come."

"No!" Brushing her tears away, she said, "I want to know what happened. Please tell me."

"Later . . ." he began.

"Neville," Meriel actually managed a watery little laugh, "you must tell me the rest, else I shall have a relapse."

Looking at her, he smiled. "Very well— in the interests of a speedy recovery—" He had driven his phaeton back along the Great North Road seeking the Hodgkins Circus. He had stopped and asked after it in every village en route. He had been to so many he had lost count, when in the late afternoon, five days after he had begun his anguished search, he rode into Norman Cross to receive the information that the circus was in Great Castleton. At Great Castleton, the following morning, he had learned that it had moved onto Grantham; in Grantham, they mentioned Cromwell.

He had caught up with it in Cromwell, but it was battened down for the night and it was not until the following morning that he had been able to visit the Oddities. There, he saw the poster emblazoned with a picture of a blue-headed mermaid. His heart had leaped in his breast, but he had to wait until noon when the exhibit opened. He'd paid his money to Mr. Swain, wincing at the sight of his brutal face. "Indeed, much as I wanted to find you, I almost prayed you'd not be in the clutches of such a rogue. Then, I went in." He paused, biting his lip. "The curtain was down. It rolled up slowly and there you were—so thin, so wan, with your vacant eyes and your strained smile. I wanted to rush down there and smash open the glass and rescue you, for I was sure you were never there of your own free will. However, I saw Swain walking back and forth and knew that tired as I was, I was no match for his strength. It was then I remembered the Great Khan."

He had sought him out and between performances, he had told him his story. At first the magician had been reluctant to aid Lord Farr, for after all, Mr. Swain was a colleague. However, he had heard vague rumors concerning Swain's ill-treatment of his new Oddity and the Pin-Headed Boy, farmed out to another exhibitor, had been in a pitiably starved condition. His wife had corroborated both rumors, adding darkly that she would not like to be in the clutches of that "hatchet faced shrew" who was wed to Swain.

However, neither had inquired deeply into the matter because they were busy with their own act and, besides, he had never liked the Swains. None of the circus folk did. They were left much to their own devices, especially since Swain had the reputation of being both a violent and a dangerous man. It was known that he had beaten one of the roustabouts nearly to death, on the excuse that the man, a burly individual himself, had attacked him. Fortunately, the Great Khan remembered Lord Farr and seeing his distress, he had taken pity on him. It was he who had concocted the Indian disguise and spread the word about that he had acquired a new assistant. "That way, you'll be able to move freely among us, for you'll be counted as one of us."

In the interests of being "one of them" Lord Farr, though chafing greatly at the delay, had actually performed with the Great Khan, and it was not until the circus had reached Berkeley Moor, eighteen miles distant, that he had been able to think of rescuing Meriel. However, during the two days he had spent with the circus, he had made inquiries and he had learned that none of the Oddities or their keepers had ever seen the mermaid strolling about the tents as the others did. Yet, none had dared inquire into the reasons for her seclusion, for all were afraid of Swain.

When he was convinced that Meriel was, indeed, a prisoner, he had persuaded the Great Khan to come to her tent to see if there was any feasible way she could be removed from her enclosure. But they found it to be impregnable. It was then that Lord Farr had concocted his scheme about the snake. In order to make the story seem authentic, he had gone to each caravan with his tale before approaching the Swains. It was while he was speaking with the man that he had managed, through slight of hand, to plant the device that had caused the odor and the smoke.

"There was no fire?" Meriel asked.

"None," he said, hastily. "Can you think I would venture to use anything so dangerous when I knew you were there? No, it was an illusion known to the Brotherhood, who use it to obtain certain stage effects. Once having accomplished my purpose, I waited until they came running out. She tripped and fell unconscious. I dashed inside and found that you were chained!" His mouth was a grim line and his eyes blazed. He fell silent again, gripped by a remembered rage.

"How did you manage to release me? He had the key," she said.

"Love and anger lent me strength. I pulled the chain from the stake and I brought you out. As I put you down, Swain rushed me."

"Ohhhh," Meriel clutched his arm, "did he hurt you?"

The grimness in his eyes intensified. "No, for I shot him."

"You d-didn't kill him!" she cried.

"Surely, you'll not be wasting pity on that miscreant," he rasped.

"I would not have you in danger of prosecution!" she replied.

"Always you will think of my welfare." He sighed. "And I am so unworthy of you, my very dearest. But be of good cheer. He is not dead. I aimed only at his arm and gave him a flesh wound that halted him before he was able to close with me."

"What happened, then? Where is he?" she asked a little fearfully.

"Safe, my love, quite safe—he and his wife lie in prison, held there on charges of abduction and cruelty."

"But how could you prove it?"

"I had the chain and manacle—and I had your poor wasted, bruised little body to describe." He swallowed convulsively and then continued. "It is said that they will be transported, though I hope their ship sinks." He paused, then he added, "Now you must promise me three things, my sweet."

"Three things?" she repeated.

"Three." He nodded.

"What are they?" she asked.

"One: you must promise me that now I have told you the whole of it, you'll put this regrettable episode from your mind as soon as possible."

"I am trying my best to do so. What else would you have of me?"

"You must never mention it again—not to anyone."

"I never, never shall," she promised. "And the third thing?"

He possessed himself of her hand again. "Can you not guess what the third thing might be, my adorable, brave, beautiful love?"

"N-No." She knew she was blushing, and seeing the look in his eyes, she felt her heart beating high in her throat. "I think you must tell me," she faltered.

"I shall not tell you," he said firmly. "I shall ask you." Dropping her hand, he rose and moving to a point directly in front of her, he knelt. "My dear Meriel," he said in a low, vibrant voice, "Since I have long cherished the very deepest affection for you, might I hope that you will do me the honor of consenting to be my wife?"

"Oh," she breathed, her hands fluttering out to stroke his face. "My dear, my dearest Lord, you must not kneel to me," she protested. Slipping from her chair, she pressed herself against him, flinging her arms around him, she said, "Yes! Oh, yes, yes, yes, yes, yes!" and would have gone on repeating that particular affirmative had not his lips come down to silence her.

# Epilogue

The great townhouse on South Street was ablaze with lights and the thoroughfare before it so jammed with carriages that it was well-nigh impossible for many conveyances to get through. Stalled coachmen cursed at each other and infuriated passengers, sticking their heads out the windows of post-chaises and coaches, wondered audibly and aggrievedly, why they were stopping. Behind them, however, other vehicles let members of the *beau monde* descend to make their joyous way toward the mansion.

Inside, a ball was in progress and on either side of the double staircase, footmen in powdered wigs, bright blue livery heavy with gold braid, silk stockings and feet thrust into patent leather shoes with glittering paste buckles stood at attendance while illustrious guests ascended the marble stairs, their vivid satins and velvets illuminated by crystal chandeliers, ablaze with hundreds of candles. Their glowing flames, reflected in dangling drops, cast dancing rainbow patterns on the walls.

At the top of the stairs, an imposing major-domo announced the arrivals in stentorian tones and no one was surprised that the Prince Regent had graced the fete with his presence. It was well known that he had already entertained the guests of honor, the Earl and Countess of Farringdon, at Carlton House and had pronounced them delightful. Indeed, as he had gone into the ballroom, his Highness was heard to say, "I must have a waltz with the Countess. Never did have a partner so light on her feet."

However, the Prince was not to have his wish granted so readily for the lady in question was not to be found in the magnificent mirrored ballroom. Instead, the more humble library was being treated to a vision in a white gown of the finest Indian muslin. The sleeves long and topped at the shoulder by tiers of lace, matched an overdress that was also of lace, lined with pale pink sarcenet in a color most appropriately called "Maiden's Blush." There was a sparkle of diamonds at the throat of this confection, and in the tiara, which was perched on her crown of short, pale golden curls. She looked lovely but a trifle wan. Lady Susan Campion, charming in pink-striped French gauze over white satin was, though not her equal in beauty, extremely pleasing to the eye. Yet, as she hovered over the Countess, her forehead was marred by a slight frown. "Lean back against the pillows, do," she said, as the lady sank down on a loveseat. "Should you like some champagne?"

"No," the Countess replied quickly. "Thank you, but champagne does not set well with me at present. I should prefer water, I think."

"I shall tell a footman to bring it to you immediately." Lady Susan whisked out the door and was back in a moment to find the Countess fanning herself. "I do hope you are not in any great discomfort."

"Oh, not at all, but it was warm in the ballroom. It is a little warm here, too, Lady Susan. I find myself more prone to feel the heat, now."

"I did, too, when I was increasing." Lady Susan smiled. "Especially during the fourth month."

The Countess flushed. "I am not quite out of my third."

There was a tap on the door. "Come in," Lady Susan called.

A footman bearing a glass of water on a silver tray entered. Taking it, Lady Susan thanked him and brought the glass to the Countess who sipped the water gratefully.

"Ah, now I do feel better. I should go back soon. Neville will be disturbed if I am gone too long."

"Oh, you need not tell me that." Lady Susan smiled. "He treats you as though you were made of blown glass. I never saw a man so considerate or, I might add, so much in love, and after a year and a half of marriage. I vow, I am quite envious."

"You need not be," the Countess chided. "It seems to me that your Norbert is quite as fond of you."

"Oh, I expect he is, but he does not show it so much. Then, I suppose, too, that it is the contrast between the old Neville and the new. I never thought he would be able to remain away from town so long."

The Countess flushed. "I am afraid he did that because of my hair."

"That might have been true in the beginning, but from the way he speaks now, he does not want to remain in town. He actually seems anxious to get back to Farringdon."

"Well"—the Countess smiled—"I expect he is. He has become quite interested in the running of the estate."

"I know!" Lady Susan laughed. "Why to hear him talk about the improvements he means to make in the tenant's cottages and so forth . . . it's quite amazing! He has grown extremely *responsible*. Earlier this evening, I reminded him of the Ball he gave in honor of the Arabian Queen, who turned out to be a mare in full evening dress and with a tiara! Can you believe that he gave me a frozen stare and the most complete set-down. Whatever has happened to his sense of humor?"

"Oh, he still possesses it," the Countess said, fondly, "but it has taken other less spectacular forms and, of course, the thought of approaching fatherhood is somewhat sobering. I think he will recover soon."

"Oh, Meriel." Lady Susan clapped her

hands. "How delightfully everything has turned out. If you but knew how happy it made me when I saw you come up the stairs in that ravishing gown, especially when I glimpsed my Step-Mama. Lord, I thought she must swell up like a toad and explode! You have grown so beautiful. No, I should not say that, for you were always lovely, but—" At that moment, the door to the library was jerked open and a petulant voice resounded through the room.

"I cannot think why you wish to depart so early, Camberwell." Looking sadly out of sorts, the Marchioness of Camberwell, was followed by the Marquess; an elderly man, who was obviously much out of countenance.

"Have you forgotten that we leave at dawn for the country?" he demanded.

"I've not forgotten," she said sulkily. "I tell you, yet again, my Lord, that I do not see why we must forsake the town so soon. Or if you want to go, why will you not let me stay in town. My Mama is willing to chaperon me."

"I have no doubt that she is—and willing, too, to spend my money on new gowns and other folderol, not to mention the extra servants she will hire."

"We ought to have more," the Marchioness complained petulantly. "The house is sadly understaffed."

"Which is why I am not going to keep it open any longer. I fear I am grown far too old for the rigors of the season."

"But—"

"We will say no more on that subject, Beatrix. My mind is made up."

"I cannot—" She suddenly broke off, flushing. For she had seen the Countess of Farringdon and Lady Susan. For a moment, there was sheer fury mirrored in her eyes, then with an effort she smiled. "My dear Lady Susan, my dear Countess, good evening. Such a lovely ball, I would fain stay longer, but Camberwell is of the opinion we must have an early start in the morning. We are to visit our northern estates." She moved hastily back toward the hall. "I must get my cloak. I will bid you farewell." Without waiting for a response, she left the room.

The Marquess, following her, gave the two young woman a weary smile. "I bid you good evening, my Ladies," he said, tiredly.

"Good evening, my Lord," they chorused, as the door closed behind him.

Lady Susan laughed. "She's led him the devil of a dance, but it seems as though he will be getting his own back. She loathes the country."

The Countess bit down a smile. "It's the first time I've seen him. He seems much too old for her."

"Oh, he is," Lady Susan agreed happily. "He has the advantage of her by some thirty-five years, but what was she to do when the Duke did not come up to scratch."

"There must have been others."

"She'd refused so many offers and her dowery is not huge. Also it was her *third* season," Lady Susan explained.

The door opened again. "Meriel!" Lord Farr, looking extremely handsome in a blue satin frock coat, a white satin waistcoat stitched

204

with silver and white satin breeches, came hurrying in. "What are you doing in the library? The Prince has been asking for you." He suddenly noticed the water glass that she still held in her hand. He paled slightly. "You are not ill?" he demanded solicitously.

"Not at all," she assured him quickly. "I was only a little warm."

"Are you sure?" he pursued, coming to stand beside her chair.

"Quite sure, my love." She smiled.

"Then come, for the Prince wishes to dance with you . . . and more important so do I."

"Yes, that is much more important," she agreed, softly. Setting her glass down, she rose and took her husband's arm. "Will you be coming back with us, Susan?" she asked.

"No, not yet." Lady Susan smiled. "I will return later."

As the Countess and her husband moved down the hall, suddenly from directly above them came a howl of rage. Startled they looked up to see a raw-boned female of uncertain years, pulling an irate lad of, perhaps, eleven, away from the third-floor landing. "The idea of coming out here in your nightshirt," she said, in deep, carrying tones. "Besides I told you to go to bed!"

"I want to see the guests and I will!" the lad shrilled.

"I say you will not!" she replied, administering a sharp box on his ear. "Now you come with me, my Lord, and I don't want to hear another sound out of you."

He opened his mouth in a startled cry,

205

which, at a fearful glare from the woman, broke off mid-howl. In another second, the pair had vanished down the corridor.

Lord Farr's old mischievous smile curved his lips. "That is Miss Holcomb. She is under my uncle's orders, I understand. It serves the little monster right."

"I would never call him a monster," the Countess reproved. "Indeed, I love him dearly."

Her Lord glared at her. "My darling, though it is in your nature to be magnanimous, I shall not allow you to forgive him. Think of the ink!"

"But I do," she told him with a gentle smile, "often. I thank God for it. For did it not bring you to me? She smiled at him tenderly and he, oblivious of anyone who might have been passing, kissed her full upon her smiling lips.

# ADVENTURE...DANGER... ROMANCE!

**SWEET BRAVADO** *by Alicia Meadowes* (89-936, $1.95)

It was not a marriage made in heaven! It was a union decreed in her will by Aunt Sophie. She planned to end the feud between two branches of her family by naming joint heirs. Valentin, Viscount of Ardsmore, and Nicole Harcourt, daughter of his disgraced uncle and a French ballet dancer, would inherit Aunt Sophie's fortune only if they married each other. And wed they did. But Aunt Sophie's plan for peace had stirred up a new battle between the fiery little French girl, who wanted love — and fidelity — from her new husband, and the virile viscount, who expected his wife to want only what he wanted to give. Fun and suspense abounds in this delightful Regency Romance featuring a warm and witty heroine and a story brimming with laughter, surprise, and True Love.